OUTSIDE THE HUMAN
AQUARIUM

MORE WILDSIDE CLASSICS

Please see www.wildsidepress.com for a complete list!

OUTSIDE THE HUMAN AQUARIUM

Masters of Science Fiction

SECOND EDITION,
Revised and Expanded

by
Brian Stableford

WILDSIDE PRESS

OUTSIDE THE HUMAN AQUARIUM

This edition published in 2006 by Wildside Press, LLC.
www.wildsidepress.com

THE MILFORD SERIES
POPULAR WRITERS OF TODAY
ISSN 0163-2469
VOLUME THIRTY-TWO

OUTSIDE the HUMAN AQUARIUM

Masters of Science Fiction

SECOND EDITION,
Revised and Expanded

by

Brian Stableford

R . REGINALD
The Borgo Press
San Bernardino, California ▫ MCMXCV

THE BORGO PRESS
Twentieth Anniversary, 1975-1995
Post Office Box 2845
San Bernardino, CA 92406
United States of America

* * · * * * * *

Library of Congress Cataloging-in-Publication Data

Stableford, Brian M.
  Outside the human aquarium : masters of science fiction / by Brian Stableford. — 2nd ed., rev. and expanded.
      p. cm. — (The Milford series. Popular writers of today, ISSN 0163-
2469 ; v. 32)
  Includes bibliographical references and index.
  ISBN 0-89370-357-5 (cloth). — ISBN 0-89370-457-1 (pbk.)
  1. Science fiction, American—History and criticism. I. Title. II. Series.
PS374.S35S72 1995   95-9971
813'.0876209—dc20   CIP

SECOND EDITION

CONTENTS

ABOUT BRIAN STABLEFORD

BRIAN MICHAEL STABLEFORD was born in Yorkshire in 1948. He taught at the University of Reading for many years, but is now a full-time writer. He has written many science-fiction and fantasy novels, most recently *The Empire of Fear*, *The Werewolves of London*, and *The Angel of Pain*. He has also contributed hundreds of biographical and critical articles to reference books on science fiction, fantasy, and horror, including both editions of *The Encyclopedia of Science Fiction*. His publications for Borgo Press include: *Outside the Human Aquarium: Masters of Science Fiction* (1995), an expanded edition of his 1981 publication; *Algebraic Fantasies and Realistic Romances: More Masters of Science Fiction* (1995); *Firefly: A Novel of the Far Future* (1994); his doctoral dissertation, *The Sociology of Science Fiction* (1987); *Masters of Science Fiction: Essays on Six Science Fiction Authors* (1981); and *A Clash of Symbols: The Triumph of James Blish* (1979). Forthcoming is: *New Gods and Seedling Stars: The Fiction of James Blish and S. Fowler Wright*, an expansion of his 1979 book; *The Sociology of Science Fiction, Second Edition*; *Yesterday's Bestsellers*; *The Devil's Party: A History of Satanic Abuse*; *Glorious Perversity: The Decline and Fall of Literary Decadence*.

INTRODUCTION

Five of the essays collected here formed the main text of Volume 32 of THE MILFORD SERIES: POPULAR WRITERS OF TODAY, which was published by Borgo Press in 1981 as *Masters of Science Fiction: Essays on Six Science Fiction Authors*. "Edmond Hamilton and Leigh Brackett: An Appreciation" had earlier appeared, in slightly different form, as "The Best of Hamilton and Brackett" in *Vector* no. 90 (November/December 1978). "Locked in the Slaughterhouse: the Novels of Kurt Vonnegut" is a slightly updated version of an article bearing the same title which had appeared in *Arena* no. 8 (September 1978); that article been written in 1976 when I was commissioned to write a series of articles on contemporary SF writers for *Science Fiction Monthly*, only one of which actually appeared before the magazine ceased publication. "Insoluble Problems: Footnotes to Barry Malzberg's Career in Science Fiction" is a slightly updated version of "Insoluble Problems: Barry Malzberg's Career in Science Fiction," which had appeared in *Foundation* no. 11-12 (March 1977). "The Metamorphosis of Robert Silverberg" had appeared in something very near to its present form in the April 1976 issue of *Science Fiction Monthly*—the only element of the projected series to reach print—although that article constituted a revised version of "The Compleat Silverberg" and "Postscript to the Compleat Silverberg" which appeared in the *Speculation* no. 31 and no. 32 (December 1972 & March 1973). "Utopia—and Afterwards: Socioeconomic Speculation in the SF of Mack Reynolds" had earlier appeared, in slightly different form, as "The Utopian Dream Revisited: Socioeconomic Speculation in the SF of Mack Reynolds" in *Foundation* no. 16 (May 1979).

Four of the five essays which have been added to the present volume—those on the work of David H. Keller, Stanley G. Weinbaum, Theodore Sturgeon, and Philip K. Dick—were written for a series called "Creators of Science Fiction," commissioned by *Interzone*, where they appeared during 1994-95. All of them are, however, thorough revisions—updated where necessary—of the essays on the relevant writers which I contributed to *Science Fiction Writers*, edited by Everett F. Bleiler (Charles Scribner's Sons, 1982). The remaining essay, on the work of Clark Ashton Smith, is a slightly revised and updated version of an essay I wrote in 1987 for a book of essays on American supernatural fiction edited by Douglas Robillard which never made it into print; it overlaps to some small degree two essays on Smith which I had pre-

5

viously written for the Bleiler *Science Fiction Writers* and for the Salem Press *Survey of Modern Fantasy Literature* (1983), edited by Frank Magill.

Most of the earlier essays reprinted here are, of course, long out of date. However, Barry Malzberg has added relatively little to his canon since his "insoluble problems" made him extremely disenchanted with the *genre*, and Mack Reynolds was unfortunately unable to add much more to the list of his own works before his death in 1983. Robert Silverberg did return to the field after a temporary withdrawal of his labor, but he had in the meantime undergone a further metamorphosis every bit as dramatic as that delineated in the essay, so this essay remains reasonably complete in describing the particular phase of his career in which it is most interested. The rather dispirited novels which Kurt Vonnegut has issued at irregular intervals since the essay included here was completed are also somewhat at variance with those described in the essay, and it might be argued that they add relatively little to the sum total of his achievements. For these reasons, I think the essays retain almost all of whatever interest they had when they first appeared, and I am content to let them remain as they are.

The early essays are the record of fascinations which were at their most fervent at the times when they were written. Although I still have a considerable affection and admiration for all the subjects concerned, any analysis of their work which I undertook now would undoubtedly be a good deal more distant. The consideration given to the authors included in the "Creators of Science Fiction" series is, indeed, more distant and more coolly contemplative—although I would not claim that it is any more "objective" in consequence. Distance has its advantages, but it has its disadvantages too; I feel that it would be a pity to impose its cool administration upon everything I write or attempt to preserve, but it would also be a pity to exclude it entirely.

—Brian Stableford
Reading, England
February 1995

I.

EDMOND HAMILTON AND LEIGH BRACKETT

AN APPRECIATION

Edmond Hamilton died on February 1, 1977 at the age of seventy-two. His wife, Leigh Brackett, died little more than a year later, on March 18th 1978. She was sixty-two. Both made their reputations writing science fiction for the pulp magazines. Hamilton began publishing in 1926 and was one of the most prolific contributors to the early SF pulps and to *Weird Tales,* his work typifying in many respects the kind of writing that emerged to supply the nascent *genre.* Brackett, in contrast, was most prolific in the period 1948-55—the period which saw the death of the pulps—and her work is redolent with a kind of nostalgia for the exotic that reflects the decline of a way of writing and a way of dreaming. Both writers, of course, adapted to the new regime of digest magazines and paperback books, but both remained irredeemably associated in the minds of the reading public with the pulps.

The SF pulps lasted barely thirty years—more than a generation but considerably less than a lifetime. In the post-war period a host of new SF writers emerged who had had little or nothing to do with the pulps, but the great majority of the pulp writers were still alive, and with a substantial amount of writing still in them. Most had been in their teens or twenties when *Amazing Stories* was founded (Hamilton was twenty-one, Brackett ten), and it is only in the present decade that their three-score-years-and-ten is running out. As a generation, they are dying now. Campbell's generation, who were recruited to the cause of *Astounding Stories* in 1938-40, are still, for the most part, alive, but they were not only of a different time but of a different species. They were never pulp writers first and foremost in the sense that the older generation was, for their first loyalty was to the Campbellian manifesto for SF (which is not to say that *Astounding* never published pure pulp adventure fiction, and certainly not to say that the older generation could write nothing but). Though Leigh Brackett made her first appearance in *Astounding* ("Martian Quest" in 1940), she is principally associated with the school of pulp writing which survived alongside it in *Startling Stories, Thrilling Wonder Stories,* and *Planet Stories.*

Hamilton published only one story in *Astounding* after Campbell assumed control ("The Ephemerae" in 1938), and he, too, was to give his principal allegiance to the SF adventure pulps, most prolifically to the SF hero-pulp *Captain Future*.

It is fashionable today to regret exactly those aspects of the history of SF as a publishing category that Edmond Hamilton and Leigh Brackett exemplify: its founding as a pulp brand-name and its survival as such in parallel to the more serious quest of Campbell's *Astounding*. It has become a cliché to speak of this developing pulp category as a "ghetto" whose memory will stigmatize modern science fiction even unto the fifth generation and perhaps forever. Modern writers tend to feel that science fiction is so injured in its cultural reputation that it cannot support them in the manner to which they would like to become accustomed—not so much in terms of money (there is a growing cadre of *nouveau riche* SF writers) but in terms of literary prestige and social respectability. It is therefore commonplace (almost *de rigueur)* in today's SF community to speak of the writers who made their home in the pulps sometimes with embarrassment, always with condescension, and once in a while with dismissive vituperation. By the standards that most contemporary SF writers would like to apply to their work, pulp fiction was bad, and the fact that its methods and conventions are still echoed is something to be deplored. There are many young readers who can still enjoy formularized pulp SF, and some old ones who can glean from renewal of acquaintance with it an echo of their adolescent imaginative virility, but otherwise it has few friends. For these reasons the welcome which has been given to Ballantine/Del Rey's 1977 issuing of *The Best of Edmond Hamilton* (edited by Brackett) and *The Best of Leigh Brackett* (edited by Hamilton) has been rather cautious, despite the sentiment aroused by the recent deaths of the writers.

It is, of course, heresy to suggest that our present criteria for judging whether fiction is good or bad are only one set out of very many. Like all commonly-held value-judgments, these criteria have the force of moral authority, which owes its power to the unthinkability which it attributes to alternatives. Commonly-held value-judgments always acquire a spurious gloss of "objectivity" and "rationality" in condemning their competitors to the realms of irrationality, stupidity, moral reprehensibility, and childishness. One consequence of this is that few people today would take the trouble to ask what there is in the work of Edmond Hamilton that made it special by the standard of assessment that its target audience used, or what there is in Leigh Brackett's exotic romances that make them exceptional among their own kind. Such questions seem to the majority to be pointless and redundant. In all probability, only someone well-known for the churlish espousal of heretical views would bother to pursue these questions, and to do so without an apology.

Reading through *The Best of Edmond Hamilton*, which contains stories published over a span of forty-two years, the aspect of Hamilton's writing which seems most striking is its directness—a kind of calculated and unrepentant *naiveté*. One exception to this is the first story in the book, "The Monster-God of Mamurth" (1926), which is both a *pastiche* and one which adopts a familiar weird story convention, the traveller's tale. It has a gloss of attempted sophistication—its prose is geared to effect, the effect being the evocation of a sense of mystery and fear of the unknown, associating the strange and distant places of the Earth with a lingering supernatural hostility that has been banished from more familiar *milieux*. This kind of mood-building is what H. P. Lovecraft claimed to be the only possible function—and hence the only commendable purpose—of a fantastic story, and "The Monster-God of Mamurth" exhibits the technique and tactics that were common to most of the writers associated with *Weird Tales*. Lovecraft had little time for the SF pulps, though some of his stories appeared there, and he considered most of their fiction to be afflicted by a hopeless crudity and misdirection of imaginative effort. The second story in *The Best of Edmond Hamilton*, "The Man Who Evolved" (1931), exemplifies in many ways the tendencies to which he objected: it is unconcerned with techniques of presentation which intrude marvels gently into the perception of the reader, or with the tactics of mood-building.

Basically, "The Man Who Evolved" is a pseudo-journalistic account of the transformations undergone by a mad scientist bathing in the radiation of a machine which allows him to undergo ontogenically the entire course of future phylogenetic evolution (applying Haeckel's law in reverse, as it were). This too is a horror story, if we are to believe the narrator, who recounts his emotions in much the same tortured terms as are used by the unfortunate protagonist of "The Monster-God of Mamurth," but it is clearly of a different species. The *Weird Tales* story takes place in a remote wilderness, mostly in darkness or twilight, its menace invisible, sensed but never clearly seen. It is essentially an appeal to the vague sense of unease that we all feel when we are in an unfamiliar environment or when our usual surroundings are cloaked by darkness so that we cannot fully trust our senses. "The Man Who Evolved," by contrast, belongs to *Wonder Stories*. It takes place here and now, witnessed by ordinary men making full use of their faculties with the aid of glaring electric light. Its miracle, too, is electrically powered. In no way does it attempt to woo the ill-formed fears already present in the mind in intimate connection with certain images or ideas, but is by contrast determinedly innovative, offering a direct challenge to the imagination by attacking it not at its weakest and most vulnerable, but in its normal state of invulnerable self-confidence. The method of attack is both blunt and exaggerated, aimed at an audience predominantly young and almost wholly unawakened to the kind of possibility with which the story attempts to startle the minds of its readers. Here

Hamilton is not attempting to deal with imaginative faculties that can be teased or gently provoked to use visionary responses already well-tutored, but with faculties which have not been accustomed to the notion involved, and which are therefore vulnerable to shock tactics.

We see this method repeated throughout the earlier stories in this collection. Even the later *Weird Tales* stories attempt to capitalize on this deliberate bluntness rather than mimicking the strategies of traditional ghost stories or the gradually-built paranoia which is Lovecraft's hallmark. Hamilton believed in a direct approach to the biggest and most outrageous ideas, and this simple belief paid off. Even a story like "Thundering Worlds" (1934), which features the preposterous notion of the nine planets setting off in convoy to escape the death of the sun and to fight for possession of a new star, has a confidence that is appealing. "The Accursed Galaxy" (1935) features the absurd premise that the reason the universe seems to us to be expanding is that all other galaxies are fleeing from ours because it is infected with the "disease" of life, but it demonstrates that absurdity is not necessarily a bad thing. Absurdity presents a challenge to reason by its very nature, and thus, if it can be entertained for even a moment, offers potential for expanding the horizons of the imagination. This is the effect that Hamilton always aimed at, and often succeeeded in achieving.

Science fiction, essentially, deals with the unreal, and all of its subject matter is to the truly determined mundane thinker absurd. It coopts its disciples and its apologists by presenting its absurdities in such a way as to cloak their offensiveness, to excuse them and to conceal them behind a mask of jargon which—because of the power which jargon has in our scientifically re-mystified world—gives them spurious plausibility. SF pretends that its adventures among ideas *might* be real, *might* be possible, and thus makes us hesitate long enough for the absurdities to have their effect and unsettle our certainty. It is, of course, the *pretense* that is important insofar as SF functions as an effective medium of communication, not any actual fidelity to the supposed bounds of possibility. The importance of this pretense results in a tension between two conflicting demands: on the one hand the demand for a good disguise, an expert masquerade by which the impossible dons the raiment of the conceivable; and on the other hand the demand for mind-opening extravagance, that ever more exciting impossibilities should be so excused and infiltrated. These two demands are in conflict precisely because the best and most wholly convincing disguises are those which need to make only the most subtle amendments to conceivability. The further one goes in pursuit of the second demand the less possible it becomes to produce a mask which will stand up to close scrutiny. There are two possible answers to this dilemma: stay in those imaginative realms which lend themselves readily to the masquerade; or exchange subtlety for deliberate and flamboyant overstatement, creating by boldness of suggestion a disguise adequate only to the moment, or perhaps only a token capitulation to the very demand for disguise, so that in a brief moment of deception in which the reader may voluntarily conspire, the task of surprising the imagination may be accomplished.

Hamilton, of course, has always preferred the latter alternative in his effective work. He parades his ideas starkly, cutting straight to the heart of his material without pause or apology. These are tactics which cannot always work, but they are tactics which often *do* work, and whose workability depends on their straightforwardness and their uncompromising frankness. They deceive only momentarily because of their obviousness—like lies which are quite transparent but which nevertheless make us hesitate because of the confidence and the sincerity with which they are offered. (We have, in today's world, become connoisseurs of the *other* kind of lie, which deceives by camouflage, making itself hardly distinguishable from truth, and it is hardly surprising that we prefer fiction of the same kind. We have come to feel that to hesitate momentarily in the face of a bold lie is somehow to be made a fool, and we are inclined to feel ashamed of it. We laugh at the earnest Churchman who wanted to send missionaries to More's Utopia, and find, with Alice, little sympathy for a chessman who could believe two or three impossible things before breakfast every day.)

Pulp SF, by and large, traded almost exclusively on shock tactics like Hamilton's. It was this trade in mind-opening impossibilities which distinguished it from other brands of pulp fiction, and made it something more than a new and bizarre variety of costume melodrama. As a literary strategy it was very much a blunt instrument, but it worked, in its way. Hamilton became exceptional among pulp writers, and a favorite of SF fans, simply because he told bigger lies than most in a fashion more barefaced than any. Ideatively he was not as prolific as Jack Williamson or as brash as Edward E. Smith and John Campbell, but he was the most open, and hence the most accessible, of all.

Because of its openness and deliberate simplicity, Hamilton's work is often close to fable. His treatment of archetypal SF themes in "The Island of Unreason" (1933), "Fessenden's Worlds" (1937), and "Day of Judgment" (1946) are possessed of the innocent panache of the fabulist, each with a moral presented rather too blandly for sophisticated literary taste. Hamilton wrote a whole series of such stories, extending from "A Conquest of Two Worlds" (1932) to "After a Judgment Day" (1963). (There are several notable examples not included in *The Best of Edmond Hamilton,* especially "Sacrifice Hit" (1954), "Sunfire!" (1962), and "The Stars My Brothers" (1962).)

The second aspect of Hamilton's writing revealed quite clearly here is in some ways a surprising one, for it calls into question one of the myths regarding pulp SF. Fans who look back to a Golden Age when Hamilton and kindred spirits were supreme among the writers of pulp SF complain of today's SF that it is too often downbeat—preoccupied with the intense conviction of the limits of human capability.

But Hamilton, at his most impressive, is constantly and almost obsessively concerned with mortality and the vanity of human wishes. "The Man Who Evolved," "In the World's Dusk" (1936), and "The Accursed Galaxy" are all frontal attacks on human self-glorification. "The Man Who Returned" (1935)—a *Weird Tales* story about a man returned from the grave to find himself very unwelcome in the land of the living—is conscientiously cynical. "He That Hath Wings" (1938), about a child born with wings whose attempt to adjust to humankind is not only unsuccessful in itself but also puts paid to his chances of being successfully different, shows a marked pessimism about the human condition which accepts no compromise.

It is true that if we take Hamilton's total wordage into account this lack of confidence in the human spirit shows through only occasionally, perpetually stifled in his longer works in favor of grandiose plotting and fast-paced action, but much of that fiction was no sooner read than forgotten, and in the novels which survive as being memorable—*The Star of Life* (1947), *The Valley of Creation* (1948), and *The City at World's End* (1950)—there is at least an echo of the same feeling. The one major exception is *The Star Kings* (1947), which is the second of Hamilton's three attempts to co-opt the plot of *The Prisoner of Zenda* into space opera, and which represents a romantic self-indulgence not altogether typical of his work. In his stories of the fifties and sixties the anti-romantic streak in Hamilton became more and more prominent. It may have appeared much earlier had the original version of "What's It Like Out There?" (1952) been published when written in 1933, but once liberated it found adequate expression. Perhaps the best of all the stories Hamilton wrote is "The Pro" (1964), whose authenticity seems guaranteed by its sincerity in the matter of a science fiction writer's realization of the gulf between the romantic aspects of his work and the reality of the conquest of space. The tension between pessimism and romanticism is nowhere better represented than in the story "Requiem" (1962), about the man who ferries interstellar tourists and sensation-seekers to watch the death of Earth.

It would be easy enough to see in Hamilton a writer of two *personas,* one of which committed merry genocide against dozens of loathsome alien invaders of Earth while the other wrote "A Conquest of Two Worlds"; one of which delighted in extravagant and lush interplanetary romances while the other wrote "What's It Like Out There?" It is easy, too, to say the same thing about his contemporaries, for Don A. Stuart seemed a very different writer from John W. Campbell Jr., and the Jack Williamson who wrote *The Legion of Space* and *The Legion of Time* is not quite the man who wrote "Star Bright" (1939) and "The Crucible of Power" (1939). This would, however, be something of a misrepresentation, for the deliberate indulgence in romanticism is usually correlated with a sober cynicism, leaning towards pessimism, relative to the real world and its prospects. An enthusiasm for the vast and distant, and for working on the fringes of imaginability, is very often the corollary of a disappointment with and a more-or-less vague distaste for the immediate and the ordinary, which can easily find expression in a more desolate vision of derelict futures. Pulp SF, unlike other pulp *genres,* has always had an uneasy affair with fantasies in which contemporary man and his world—especially his cherished values and prejudices—come to grief. This is evident even in Hamilton's work of the early pulp days, despite its ideative exuberance and its lust for unsubtle excitement, and it comes to dominate the work which he did for the pulps in their twilight. It is thus not surprising to find that in Leigh Brackett's work, which is virtually archetypal of the senescence of the pulp SF tradition, it has its equivalent, and that that equivalent is very much the heart of her work.

The Best of Edmond Hamilton contains twenty-one stories, and follows the usual pattern of avoiding long novelettes in favor of short stories. *The Best of Leigh Brackett,* in contrast, contains only ten stories (despite being forty pages longer). Brackett's good work was virtually all done in the range from 10,000-45,000 words—her better novels are her shorter ones: *The Sword of Rhiannon* (originally "Sea Kings of Mars"), *Shadow Over Mars* (also known as *The Nemesis from Terra), The Secret of Sinharat* (originally "Queen of the Martian Catacombs"), and *People of the Talisman* (originally "Black Amazon of Mars"). Those which were expanded for book publication gained little in the padding.

Brackett once left a story incomplete to be finished by Ray Bradbury, and though she and Bradbury now stand poles apart in the matter of their literary reputation, they have in common that between them they worked out the post-Burroughsian image of mythical Mars. Both used the tension which existed between Burroughs's fantasy Mars and the astronomical evidence which has eroded Lowell's speculations and brought the fantasy under sentence of death.

Burroughs himself saw Mars as a decadent planet, already ancient, its life ebbing slowly away. Both Brackett and Bradbury accentuated that image, producing a Mars *more* ancient, *more* decadent, facing oblivion. In this they were right, for mythical Mars was, indeed on the brink of death as the slender thread of hopeful possibility was severed forever by the march of twentieth century knowledge. *The Martian Chronicles* is already securely established as a period piece, and Brackett, when she returned for the second time from scripting films to writing SF in the seventies, was forced to forsake the *milieux* which had made her early reputation. (The folly of trying to trade on nostalgia alone is amply demonstrated by Lin Carter's sadly incongruous Brackett *pastiches.*)

Not all of Brackett's novelettes are set on Mars, but her fantasy Venus and her fantasy Mercury are simple linear extensions of Martian mythology. The names vary little in tone, and though the landscapes participate in different exotic features, the same sense of eroded environment and planetary senescence is ever-present, because it is essential.

In his introduction to *The Best of Leigh Brackett,* her husband identifies a "favorite and recurring theme" in her work, which he describes as "the theme of a strong man's quest for a dream and of his final failure when it turns to smoke and ashes in his hand...her heroes seek for something they can never quite attain, yet their failure is not really defeat." This is accurate in its way, but misleading in its emphasis. It misses the point, which is that Brackett's stories carry a consistent moral: that the pursuit of dreams is ultimately and essentially a pointless pursuit, for even when they are caught they are illusions that can only deceive. Brackett is constantly fascinated by the allure of the exotic, and becomes fascinating in her own work through her dedicated attempt to represent that allure, but she is also constantly suspicious of its temptations and always certain that victory lies not in capturing dreams, but in having the courage to turn back again after having caught them.

In "The Jewel of Bas" (1944), the immortal Bas lives alone in his dreams while his android creations work to destroy him. When awakened to counter the menace and to free the slaves which his androids have assembled, he does what he must and then returns thankfully to his eternal dream. Meanwhile, the human characters of the story are convinced that they have the better deal in life and mortality.

In "The Veil of Astellar" (1944), a man made immortal by alien invaders lures spaceships to their doom so that he and his kind can prey upon the life force of their passengers. When he finds one of his own descendents aboard a captured ship, however, he revolts against his endless and unnatural dream life and destroys himself and his masters.

In "The Moon That Vanished" (1948), three humans sail into the moonfire, where any man can create his own reality and live in a substantial dreamworld where he is effectively a god. Two of them, though, choose to return because the very wholeness of the illusion renders it worthless. This is perhaps the best (and most fevered) story in the book, displaying the fight against temptation at its most desperate. The hero does not achieve his dream, but he wins his fight to forsake it, and that is the important thing. The same thing happens in many other Brackett stories, though not quite so obviously. In other stories in this collection there is also a reversal of the pattern, when men in mundane settings find their lives invaded by alien visions, and these show the other side of the coin, for while the heroes that live on fantasy Mars have the strength to overcome its attractions, men whose everyday lives are ordinary find the allure far less resistible. The heroes of "The Woman from Altair" (1951), "The Tweener" (1954), and "The Queer

Ones" (1956) do manage to resist successfully, but there is no real victory in their resistance, rather a heavy sense of irony.

Brackett was perhaps the gaudiest of all the SF pulp writers, and at times her purple prose almost rivals that of Merritt in its sickly luxuriance:

> It was dawn now.
>
> For a moment Heath lost all sense of time. The deck lifting lightly under his feet, the low mist and dawn over the Sea of Morning Opals, the dawn that gave the sea its name. It seemed that there had never been a Moonfire, never been a past or a future, but only David Heath and his ship and the light coming over the water.
>
> It came slowly, sifting down like a rain of jewels through the miles of pearlgrey cloud. Cool and slow at first, then warming and spreading, turning the misty air to drops of rosy fire, opaline, glowing, low to the water, so that the little ship seemed to be drifting through the heart of a fire-opal as vast as the universe.
>
> The sea turned color, from black to indigo streaked with milky bands. Flights of the small bright dragons rose flashing from the weed-beds that lay scattered on the surface in careless patterns of purple and ochre and cinnabar and the weed itself stirred with dim sentient life, lifting its tendrils to the light.
>
> For one short moment David Heath was completely happy.

But one short moment it is—a brief dalliance, a submission to glamour that cannot and does not last. It is thus that Brackett differs from Merritt—in Merritt's work the glamourous illusion is the one and only goal; his characters are wholehearted in their longing to escape into dreams, and if they are turned back (they never turn back of their own accord), their return to reality is stark tragedy. When Merritt had the hero of *The Dwellers in the Mirage* expelled from his glorious hallucination, it constituted a downbeat ending of such emotional ferocity that the editor of *Argosy* refused to tolerate it and rewrote it (the original version appeared only in the reprint magazine *Fantastic Novels*). Merritt genuinely was an *escapist*, who despaired in real life precisely because his wonderful dreams were quite unattainable. Brackett's fascination with the exotic, however, was by no means such an unreasoned infatuation. She was, paradoxical as it may seem, an *anti-romantic* writer; not because she determinedly affected "realism" (though she *could* maintain such an affectation, as in her thrillers), but because she persistently denied the real value of the insistent temptations of her fantasies. Among her later work are several stories—especially "The Last Days of Shandakor" (1952) and the last of her Martian stories, "The Road to Sinharat" (1963)—whose manifest subject matter is the death of dreams and the crushing of the ancient and the exotic by the irresistible pressure of time and common sense.

Brackett, like Bradbury, was an essentially nostalgic writer, and her nostalgia likewise found as one of its principal imaginative *milieux* the Burroughsian Mars that seemed so bright and real in her childhood. In her stories, though, the nostalgia is constantly accompanied by a ghostly awareness that the myths and fantasies of childhood cannot and should not be sustained, but saved for transient moments of self-indulgence. This she finds sad, but she does not (as Hamilton implies) represent the impossibility at capturing dreams as a kind of failure; rather it is a kind of success. Her work, which stands at the end of the SF pulp tradition, is orientated backwards in time, constituting in large measure a reflection upon that tradition insofar as it served the escapist needs of its readers. In her way she was as little committed to the wilder excesses of this escapist need as—on close inspection—Hamilton turns out to have been. That is what made both of them *science fiction* writers rather than fantasists. They both owed allegiance to the *weltanschauung* of modern rationalism, and were significantly divorced in the spirit of their writing from the fantastic imagination of writers like Burroughs, Merritt, and Cummings, whose work resembles theirs in superficial symbology, but which is irredeemably committed to the flight from reason.

Edmond Hamilton and Leigh Brackett do not belong to the science fiction of today. Their work forms part of a tradition now virtually extinct. This is largely because we live in a different period of history. In the twenties and thirties Hamilton's literary strategies were effective, because there was at that time a large audience whose scientific and science-fictional *naiveté* was undefiled. There is no such audience today, because even those people who are just beginning to read SF in their teens have already been familiarized with most of the ideas that were new and mind-expanding to the similar generation of 1926. The mythology of SF has slowly permeated the cultural atmosphere. Similarly, the kind of childhood fantasy from which Brackett's work is one important stage removed no longer has the dominance over present-day juvenile literary experience that it once had. Despite these facts, however, the best stories of Edmond Hamilton and the best stories of Leigh Brackett do have a certain timelessness. They will not appeal on the same wide scale even to today's emergent SF community, but there will always be something that they have to offer a particular type of reader: the reader who *does* find it possible to achieve that momentary hesitation which allows a wild idea to sting his imagination; or the reader who *has* found himself quite entranced by the allure of ultra-exotic dreams. Because this is so it is not necessary to justify an interest in these two writers by considering their work as period pieces. They can both be recommended as good and special writers.

II.

LOCKED IN THE SLAUGHTERHOUSE

The Novels of Kurt Vonnegut

Kurt Vonnegut, Jr. has successfully defied classification as a science fiction writer, although four of his novels and about a dozen of his short stories are science fictional in content. Some ambitious SF writers who feel themselves entrapped by the label have drawn an unfair correlation between Vonnegut's success and his escape from categorization, and have hinted that Vonnegut's defiance arose from shrewd commercial instinct.

The fact is, however, that Vonnegut has established his uniqueness as a writer, so that the generic label becomes less informative with respect to his work than the label of his own name. There is a unity in his novels which makes them all a coherent whole irrespective of the fact that some use ideas derived from SF's characteristic vocabulary while some do not.

Most SF writers are collaborators in a collective endeavor, participants in the building of a mythological edifice concerned with finding roles for man in an infinite but reified universe. Vonnegut is not primarily a contributor to the mythology of SF (although one of his characters, Kilgore Trout, most certainly is). His concerns are more individual, and more specific.

Vonnegut's fiction first began to appear regularly in 1950. Although a good proportion of his early short stories were science fiction, they were mostly published outside the SF establishment—several were in *Collier's*. At about this time *The Magazine of Fantasy & Science Fiction* was beginning to import the conventions of "slick" writing into the *genre* (all of whose outlets had previously been governed by the conventions of pulp writing), but Vonnegut did not appear in *F&SF* until 1961. A couple of short stories which presumably "fell through" the slick market ended up in *Galaxy* in 1953-54. All of this early material, SF or not, tended to be suavely satirical. Most of the ideas contained in the stories were bogged down by the showy glibness which the market demanded, and it is perhaps significant that the most sharply satirical of them were the two that ended up in *Galaxy*: "Unready to Wear" and an abridged version of "Tomorrow and Tomorrow and Tomorrow" (as "The Big Trip Up Yonder").

Player Piano, Vonnegut's first novel, was roughly contemporary with these two short stories. It is, like them, more direct and aggressive than the slick fiction. It has been described (as have many other futuristic anti-Utopias) as a satire, but this description is inaccurate. We have, in fact, no word to identify this kind of exercise. Satire is a literary form which seeks to ridicule aspects of contemporary life by grotesque exaggeration. Because of this exaggeration, tending always to absurdity, satire often becomes fantastic—but this does not mean that all fantasies of exaggeration are satires. In science fiction of the variety to which *Player Piano* belongs (as do *Brave New World, Messiah, The Space Merchants*, etc.), the exaggeration arises by extrapolation from a hypothetical premise or set of premises. Its purpose is to explore the implications of the premises in a dramatic manner, and while the extent of the extrapolation may, indeed, result in *reductio ad absurdum*, the primary intention is not to make the premises seem ridiculous.

Player Piano does not seek to make its premises ridiculous, but to show that they are dangerous. To call it satire is to trivialize it unjustly. The novel's concern is the slow destruction of human quality and purpose by the progressive surrender of all human actions and decisions to machines. This is, of course, the concern of a great deal of fifties' SF (and of some of the most interesting stories produced in the thirties and forties), but *Player Piano* is untypical because of its method.

One aspect of that method is the simple fact that Vonnegut escaped (because he had never been involved with) the assumptions of pulp writing. *Player Piano* is wordy, unmelodramatic, and carefully pedestrian. Rather more important, however, is the odd texture of the prose. There is considerable wit—the whole tone is ironic—but no comedy. A sequence of scenes outside the main narrative thread concerns the travels of a visiting sheik who persistently fails to comprehend the miracle of technological democracy, and persists in thinking of the citizens of the United States as slaves. This irony is not intended to be humorous. It is, instead, presented as evidence of the insanity of the tragedy.

This is perhaps the most remarkable feature of Vonnegut's writing: as his career progressed this irony came more and more to the fore, and his most recent novels contain little else. His work often tends toward the blackest of black comedy, but rarely employs wit for its own sake or for more amusement. Vonnegut is no clown, and those who find his work funny are apt to be missing the point.

The hero of *Player Piano* is Paul Proteus, a man who enjoys all the advantages that the super-technological state can offer to the favored few who still have a vital role to play within it. The story is an account of how and why he comes to find it all quite intolerable, and finally joins the revolution.

This is not by any means an original plot, but the book's chief virtue is that it makes clear what most comparable novels produced within the SF establishment could only say metaphorically: that rebellion against technological progress has to take place in the head, not in the streets—that it is a revolution which must be thought rather than fought. In pulp-ancestral SF, committed to action rather than idea, the hero has to tear down the hypothetical world he rejects, expressing the failure of the thought-experiment with gaudy violence and the symbolic slaughter of draconian scapegoats. The necessity of the form can often weaken the whole experiment, especially in that the identification and accusation of scapegoats is always too easy an answer to any problem.

In *Player Piano* the revolution never has a chance—it is the fact that it takes place at all which is significant. More significant still—especially in the context of Vonnegut's subsequent work—is the fact that there is no scapegoat to gather and accept the blame. One of the most impressive things about Vonnegut's stories is that they *never* use villains. He has always refused to employ the ritual exorcism of evil which people of all cultures, in all the manifold forms of cultural and artistic expression, have found, throughout history, all-too-convenient.

The *enemy* in *Player Piano* (and all the other novels) is not a man or a machine, but an assumption manifest as a belief. The particular one under attack here is voiced by Proteus as follows:

> You perhaps disagree with the antique and vain notion of Man's being a creation of God.... But I find it a far more defensible belief than the one implicit in intemperate faith in lawless technological progress—namely that man is on earth to create more durable and efficient images of himself, and, hence, to eliminate any justification at all for his own existence. (Chapter XXX)

Vonnegut's work in general is replete with what, for want of an English word, we may call *weltschmerz*. *Chambers* defines the word (borrowed from the German) ambiguously as "sympathy with universal misery" and "thoroughgoing pessimism." The ambiguity is, I think, what makes the word useful. *Player Piano* has both pessimism and sympathy, and the unfunny irony arises almost entirely from this contradiction in feeling. Although some short stories by Vonnegut show only sentimental sympathy or cruel pessimism, in the novels the two are always co-existent and always inextricably interlinked.

A gap of six years separated publication of *Player Piano* (1953) and *The Sirens of Titan* (1959). *Sirens of Titan* and the two novels which followed it (*Mother Night* in 1961 and *Cat's Cradle* in 1963) are all works of considerable artistry, and it is tempting to put them forward as his best work. However, they are not quite the same *kind* of work as the later novels, especially *God Bless You, Mr. Rosewater* (1965), *Slaughterhouse-5* (1969), and *Breakfast of Champions* (1973), and perhaps ought not to be directly compared with them. The earlier novels each have a structural unity which the later novels lack, for the second group of novels have little structural organization and their content (including their characters) overflows and intermingles.

The second group of three novels really have to be read *in context*, and have little independence, like bees within a hive. This confers certain virtues: sections of prose can be stripped down to the bare essentials with the external "climate of thought" supplying much of the meaning, thus giving the work a deceptive simplicity. Necessarily, though, the later novels lack the internal strength of the earlier ones, and if one takes Vonnegut's books one at a time (which may not be the best way to take them), *The Sirens of Titan* is undoubtedly the most impressive.

The hero of the book is Malachi Constant, who is guilty of no less a sin than taking his good luck for granted. He is fond of saying: "Somebody Up There Likes Me." He is wrong, and the entire hypothetical universe of the book is dedicated to *proving*, to him and to everyone else, that he is wrong. The whole plot and background are designed to expose the absurdity of the vain belief that luck is the hand of the Almighty.

The character who turns the wheels of the plot is Wilson Niles Rumfoord, who—owing to a *contretemps* with a chronosynclastic infundibulum—has been distributed through spacetime in a curious manner. He materializes periodically on Earth and Mars while being permanently materialized on Titan. Because his viewpoint is to a degree external to the time-scheme of the book, he has an odd kind of objectivity: because he knows what is going to happen, his own active role in events is already defined for him. This use of an extratemporal viewpoint, from which all moments appear co-existent, is important in *Slaughterhouse-5*, which has strong ideative links with *The Sirens of Titan*.

Rumfoord organizes a hopeless Martian invasion of Earth which becomes a massacre, and in its emotional aftermath he establishes the Church of God the Utterly Indifferent, in whose doctrine Malachi Constant becomes a kind of devil. In the meantime, to prove to Malachi that nobody "up there" really gives a damn about him, Rumfoord has him shanghaied to Mars, forces him to murder his only friend, mates him to his own (Rumfoord's) ex-wife, and finally ships him off to Titan where the whole thing is cruelly explained. The embittered

Rumfoord's tampering with human destiny turns out to be as nothing, however, compared to that which has happened on a much greater time-scale. Also on Titan is Salo, a shipwrecked Tralfamadorian, who has been waiting for a replacement part for his spaceship while his own "people" have developed the human race as a device for communication with him. The ruthless attack on human vanity reaches its ultimate end when Salo decides to find out what his mission is, to discover what end the manipulation of the human race has served. His message is just a single dot, a greeting from the Tralfamadorians to another race in another part of the universe.

Science fiction, by virtue of its very nature, sets human existence in a context far greater than that provided by the "mainstream" novel. It is not the only literature to have used a cosmic perspective, but it is the one which employs the particular cosmic perspective provided by scientific knowledge and the scientific imagination. What individual writers see when they set characters on a stage which is potentially infinite in both space and time varies a good deal. Edward E. Smith discovered in the vast new universe a gigantic playground for adventures in make-believe. Alfred Jarry discovered such vastness that all human pretension and ambition became patently absurd. H. P. Lovecraft discovered a universe so vast and so alien as to be utterly horrifying. A. E. van Vogt discovered realms of possibility so extensive that anyone might be a latent superman or a potential demigod. Vonnegut saw man in the cosmic setting as a helpless creature whose attempts to discover his own purpose and meaning were futile, because on a stage so vast there could not *be* any purpose or meaning.

The conclusion of *The Sirens of Titan* is that if the real purpose of mankind may not to be to relay messages to a stranded Tralfamadorian, then it might as well be. If God does not exist, inventing him becomes an endorsement of his Utter Indifference.

Vonnegut has closer ties with Jarry and Lovecraft than with Smith or van Vogt. But while Jarry was content to dramatize his feeling that it was all absurd, and Lovecraft was content to dramatize his feeling that it was all utterly horrible, Vonnegut went further. He was not merely cynically pessimistic, but also sympathetic toward the prisoners of the derelict universe, his fellow men.

His next novel, *Mother Night,* explores the difficulties of trying to find a purpose in a purposeless existence. Its lead character, Howard W. Campbell Jr., is an American ex-Nazi who has been both a propagandist for Hitler and an American spy. His problem is simply to discover which was (and which remains) his "true" identity. The trouble is that he found it so simple to be both—he accepted each role quite naturally, and found them both childishly easy. He has always found it just as easy to live his overt existence as his covert one, and his conscience has never really interfered to the extent of informing him that one or the other might be evil.

The other characters in the book are no help to him, for he feels sympathy for them all. They all seem rather unreasonable and rather ridiculous, no matter which side of the fence they stand, and he hesitates to condemn any one of them. But if everyone is innocent, where did all the evil come from? What caused the slaughter and the hatred of the Second World War? Neither Campbell nor Vonnegut can find an answer. Instead, they discover a moral: "We are what we pretend to be, so we must be careful what we pretend to be." Campbell hangs himself (for "crimes against myself"), and Vonnegut went on to explore some more possibilities.

The moral of *Mother Night* may not have been much comfort to Campbell, but it was, in fact, rather hopeful. If we are what we pretend to be, then what should we pretend to be? May we not escape from the trap of purposelessness and meaninglessness with a concerted and carefully-designed system of pretence?

Well, perhaps. *Cat's Cradle* features a confrontation between two different attitudes in life. These attitudes are incarnated in two characters who exist almost entirely outside the plot, but whose ideas preside over the attempts of all the active characters to find some sense in it all. On one side of the argument is Dr. Felix Hoenikker, one of the fathers of the atom bomb and inventor of Ice-9, potential destroyer of the world. His opposite number is Bokonon, architect of a religion consisting entirely of unashamed lies, designed to make life endurable to its believers even in the most extreme circumstances. The contest is refereed by God the Utterly Indifferent, who maintains his traditional position of aloof neutrality and allows the deterministic pattern of reality to proceed according to its habit.

To Hoenikker all problems are scientific. Given a technical problem his mind works instinctively to solve it. Asked to figure out a way to freeze a battlefield so that infantrymen won't have to get bogged down in the mud, he comes up with Ice-9. It will freeze battlefields. It will also destroy the world, but that's a side effect outside the scope of the problem. To Hoenikker, all questions are theoretical. Asked by a fellow scientist whether scientists might not have sinned in discovering the atom bomb, he replies: "What is sin?"

Bokonon's approach to all problems is strictly practical. The *validity* of notions becomes inconsequential—what matters is whether they help people to get along in life. Bokononism draws its central idea from Charles Atlas, and its doctrine is earnestly ridiculous. On the small island where it thrives it is outlawed, and the penalty for believing in it is death. Everyone, including the executioner, is a secret Bokononist; the element of defiance is essential to its usefulness. In order that life may be tolerable, according to Bokonon, it must be lived in defiance of the circumstances provided by God the Utterly Indifferent.

In the plot the great falsehood loses out. Ice-9 is too real. Once its existence is hypothesized there is no way it can be contained. Even Bokonon gets frozen, but he sees to it that he freezes in the position which suits him best: thumbing his nose at the aloofly neutral referee.

The Sirens of Titan, *Mother Night*, and *Cat's Cradle* all end with someone dying, and in the manner of their dying we may perceive something of the progression of thought which runs through them. Malachi Constant dies a merciful death, comforted by an illusion provided by the sympathetic and apologetic Salo. Howard Campbell commits suicide because he can discover no such illusion. Bokonon dies defiantly, having done everything in his power to *create* such an illusion. The first novel is a book of revelation, the second is primarily analytical, and the third is creative.

Vonnegut's next three novels take for granted the conclusions of the previous three. They are disorganized, consisting of short passages drifting like flotsam in an oceanic context of thought. All the characters live in a hostile world, victims of an existential trap. There is no escape, but by defiance and determination they can still come out winners, of a sort. The three novels present an unremittingly downbeat view of the human condition, but they are all—in a sense—optimistic. They marvel at the fact that there can be any hope at all, and are extravagant (if heavily ironic) in their enthusiasm for the strategies which allow something to be salvaged from the ongoing catastrophe.

In *God Bless You, Mr. Rosewater*, Eliot Rosewater, multimillionaire, becomes the only person in the world to be free of the disease of *samaritrophia*. *Samaritrophia* is the disease from which Howard Campbell suffered so much in *Mother Night*—it is the pathological suppression of an active conscience by the rest of the mind. One of its chief symptoms is Enlightened Self-Interest. It is a very useful disease, and the doctor who defines it points out that the last thing any sensible person would do is try to cure it. The unafflicted Rosewater devotes himself to giving away money and participating wholeheartedly in the activities of the Voluntary Fire Service (the only social institution he can discover which consists of people unselfishly helping one another). His enemies conspire to prove him insane, and look to have a very good case.

As Rosewater heads for the confrontation with his accusers he imagines himself caught up in a great holocaust—the firestorming of a city—and his retreat from real life becomes total for a while. In a supremely happy ending, however, he recovers and finds a way to give all his money away.

The vision of the firestorm experienced by Rosewater is a particularly significant one. In the spring of 1945 American bombers annihilated the population of Dresden and razed the city by firestorm.

They sowed a great circle of incendiary bombs, creating a tower of hot air which, in rising, created powerful winds to suck the fire inwards. Within the area the temperature rose so high that everything above ground level was destroyed and almost everything below was roasted. 135,000 people—mostly civilians, for Dresden was in no sense a military target—were killed. Among the few survivors was a group of American prisoners-of-war who were lodged in an underground cooler which had once been used for the storage of freshly-slaughtered meat. Kurt Vonnegut was one of them.

Ever since he first became a writer, Vonnegut had intended to write a book about the Dresden Holocaust, but it was not until 1969 that he managed it. The reason for this is probably that no such book could be written until he had first established the context of thought in which such an event could take its place.

That the firestorming of Dresden was an experience such as few men have lived through hardly needs to be emphasized. Vonnegut was close at hand when 135,000 people were deliberately destroyed. He worked afterwards excavating corpses. He lived in the closest possible association with the event and its consequences. From such a situation it is very difficult to find an answer to the question of why it happened. The answers which other people have found convenient (that it was justifiable as a reprisal for Nazi atrocities) were obviously inadequate to Vonnegut. His total lack of the scapegoat-seeking mentality which others find so natural may be correlated with the fact that the experience of the Dresden firestorm was far too powerful to be accomodated so easily. In order to find a context for such a monumental event some kind of cosmic perspective was necessary. (One may conjecture that Vonnegut developed his cosmic perspective not to discover a meaning for the event, but rather to discover a viewpoint from which it could be *stripped* of its meaning and fitted into the narrative of an everyday life.)

Billy Pilgrim, hero of *Slaughterhouse-5,* survives the firestorming of Dresden because he is locked in a slaughterhouse. But the firestorm fills only a few transient moments in a life which extends a long way into the time after and before the event. There are other events which have to be fitted into the same worldview which includes the firestorm: the shooting of one of his co-survivors for the alleged theft of a teapot, the plane crash which he alone survives, the tragically ridiculous death of his wife.

Billy is unstuck in time, and has to make sense of these things all at once. He cannot take them one at a time, wrap them up, and forget them. But there *is* an answer. He is kidnapped by Tralfamadorians who take him through a timewarp, abstracting him from his life temporarily to put him in a zoo with a blue movie star. To the Tralfamadorians all moments co-exist. The entire spacetime pattern of the universe is already established and unalterable. Their solution to the problem of existence is to live in the moments that are pleasant and not in the moments which are unbearable.

In a novel whose subject matter is so deadly serious the invocation of Tralfamadorians and Montana Wildhack (the movie star) seems absurd and irreverent. But this is the whole point. In order to come to terms with the reality of such things as the Dresden firestorm, nothing short of the most defiant absurdity, the most extravagant of fantasies, will do. The good moments, where life is to be lived, must be created. There is no point in waiting for them to happen, trusting to the luck that we may accidentally confuse with the hand of God. Reality, according to Vonnegut, is too hostile to permit thinking, feeling beings to be happy. Only defiant fantasies in calculated opposition to the tyranny of truth can secure a few moments worth living in.

This is the logic behind Vonnegut's celebration of Kilgore Trout, the mistreated science fiction writer. Trout, unappreciated by the world at large, is Eliot Rosewater's favorite author, becomes the only author that Billy Pilgrim can bear to read, and is the chief reason for the existence of the next Vonnegut novel, *Breakfast of Champions*.

Science fiction critics love to quote a passage from Chapter 2 of *God Bless You, Mr. Rosewater*, in which a drunken Rosewater gate-crashes a science fiction convention and showers the assembly with extravagant emotional praise. They are not so fond of quoting the comment which closes the passage a few pages later, when Vonnegut observes that what Kilgore Trout and pornography have in common is that both present "fantasies of an impossibly hospitable world." That, for Vonnegut, may not be the purpose of SF writers, but it may be all that most of it is useful for. Only in the crazy stories of Kilgore Trout can Vonnegut's characters find plausible excuses for the world's being the way it is.

This is the whole core of *Breakfast of Champions*. Dwayne Hoover, in the process of cracking up completely under the intolerable strain of trying to make sense of his life, is "saved" by reading Trout's novel *Now It Can Be Told*, which takes the form of a letter from the Creator of the Universe to the only creature possessed of free will. The whole horrible, arbitrary mess, explains the Creator, is an experiment to find out how the creature with free will reacts. This explains everything, so far as Hoover is concerned. He now knows why nothing makes sense. It is not a very satisfactory answer (he goes insane and starts attacking everyone in sight, including Trout), but it is an answer of sorts—and the only sort he is ever likely to find. All the peripheral characters in *Breakfast of Champions* live tragic lives, sustained only by the blatantly false but wholly necessary fantasies they invent for the purpose. The novel is perhaps best regarded as an extensive footnote to *Slaughterhouse-5*, reinforcing the idea of the absurdity of it all and adding an extra measure of ironic pessimism to counterbalance the extreme sympathy with which Vonnegut presented Billy Pilgrim.

There is a haggard cliché alleging that much Art is correlated with suffering. It may be as well, at the risk of sounding pretentious, to point out that such Art does not arise *directly* out of suffering but out of the attempt, conscious or unconscious, to fit a knowledge of suffering into the scheme of life. Such works as *War and Peace* do not arise by some miraculous creative process out of the *experience* of war and peace, but out of the intellectual compulsion to try and make some *sense* of the experience of war and peace. If Vonnegut is outstanding among the writers of his generation, it is not because he lived through Dresden, or because he is blessed with some mysterious and supernatural "talent," or because he has cunningly deluded the critics as to his status with regard to science fiction. It is because he has tried very hard to find a worldview compatible with what he has known and seen, and to create that worldview within a fictional *milieu*. The answers which he has raised up to supply his questions are grotesque and are presented with heavy irony, but they are not ideative whimsies intended to amuse, nor are they satire.

The works of Kurt Vonnegut are the works of an incompletely unhappy man: a man whose experience in Dresden might have shattered all faith he ever had in life or humanity, but who somehow retains an essential sympathy.

After *Breakfast of Champions* Vonnegut published several minor novels, and had a hand in the production of the television program *Between Time and Timbuktu*, which skipped lightly through some scenes extracted from his novel and from his play, *Happy Birthday, Wanda June*. Philip José Farmer also wrote a Kilgore Trout novel, *Venus on the Half-Shell*, which enjoyed some success, but is no more than a literary joke. Vonnegut's work throughout this period seems dispirited relative to his novels up to and including *Slaughterhouse-5*. The bitter comedy seems more fractious and often forced: the creative energy and moral fury that sustained him through his most impressive books seems to have been dissipated by the writing of the book that he had so long intended to write—the story of the Dresden firestorm. It remains to be seen whether he can find a new purpose which will generate new energy and channel it in such a way as to make the best use of his ability. Even if he cannot, he will be remembered as having made an important contribution to twentieth-century American literature.

III.

INSOLUBLE PROBLEMS

BARRY MALZBERG'S
CAREER IN SCIENCE FICTION

In his first collection of short science fiction stories, *Final War and Other Fantasies*, Barry Malzberg (then writing as "K. M. O'Donnell") made the following declaration:

> I believe that the future of literature, to the extent that literature does have a future...resides in science-fiction.... The literary market has become exhausted, desiccated, killed by imitation, irrelevance and the very possible running out of all the basic approaches; it flourishes now only through occasional masterpieces by writers transcending their form, but seems to have fallen, overall, on evil days. This is not true of science-fiction, where I think it can be truly said that 98% of the available material and implications which could concern a writer have not been touched.

That was probably written in 1968 (the book was published in 1969). Eight years later, Barry Malzberg quit science fiction writing because a career in science fiction, he stated, makes demands upon a writer which are, so far as he is concerned, intolerable. He was not the only one to have made such an announcement during the last few decades. Malzberg found that a large sector of the science fiction audience has little or no sympathy with the way in which he has sought to use its symbols in order to exploit that vast potential which he once saw in it.

In the opening chapters of his book *Galaxies*, where he attempts to explain why *Galaxies* is the sort of book it is rather than the sort of book he might have preferred to write, or the sort of book it might have pretended to be, Malzberg describes science fiction:

> Science fiction is not a series of working models
> for the future but merely a sub-genre of romantic fic-

tion which employs the future as historicals would use the past, as westerns would use the West, as pornography would use fornication—in short, "as a convention.

In *Galaxies* a ship falls into a black hole of galactic mass. The idea comes from articles written by John W. Campbell, Jr. On this basis, the book qualifies as "hard" science fiction. It is not, however, the kind of "hard SF" that people who like "hard SF" tend to like. The author observes that:

> Science fiction...has best been known for its simple and melodramatic plots which demonstrate man's mastery (or, later on, loss of control) of technology. The conventions of the *genre* thus demand that the novel pivot upon the attempts of the crew to leave this entrapment and return to their planet of origin...
> The problem-solving pivot is not one which I might attempt given my own devices. I am not a problem-solver by profession, let alone in my personal life. Left to myself I would be more interested in showing how the ship's inhabitants and cargo adjust to their new dwelling, how they set up light housekeeping in this unknown and difficult sector of the universe, but this would not do for the purposes of the science fiction novel. We must compete with, sell on the racks against, *The Rammers of Arcturus*.

The notion of competition here is important—in fact, it is crucial to the understanding of Malzberg's dissatisfaction with science fiction as a medium of communications. Competition means competing for an audience, and the "winners" in such a competition are the books that the largest component of that audience expects, and what it has come to demand. And what SF is all about, in terms of audience expectancy and demand, has very little to do with the kind of imaginative exploration which Malzberg once wanted to carry out.

"Science fiction," he states, again in the opening pages of *Galaxies*, "is *technological fiction*; it is an attempt to relieve anxieties about the encroaching machinery by showing people how machinery may be usefully applied."

As a statement of the social role of science fiction (that is to say, the manner in which science *fiction* is used by its readers), this is over-simplified, but it does serve to point out the fact that in today's world there tends to be an ever-widening gulf between what writers think literature should be used for and what readers actually *do* use it for.

It is not difficult to see why Malzberg has come to find science fiction a frustrating medium in which to work, in that his purpose as a writer is almost diametrically opposite to the purpose for which, in his judgment, readers seek to use his work. Malzberg's fiction explores anxiety, using the symbolic vocabulary of science fiction to characterize and dramatize the state of alienation and uncertainty into which people are driven by the acceleration of historical change and the forces of evolving technology. He deals not with solutions (whose effect, despite their imaginary nature, tends to be reassuring) but with compromises—with attempts (necessarily desperate) by individuals to adjust themselves to the terrifying awareness that the problems *may not have* "solutions." Insofar as the reader expects to find in Malzberg's work a pleasant romp through a hospitable hypothetical world where all menaces are overcome with convenient sleight-of-mind and a *machina-ex-deo*, he is likely to be not merely disappointed but positively offended. From the writer's viewpoint, this is quite some problem. What is worse is that it seems to be a problem without a solution—a problem which can only be fruitfully explored for potential compromises. *Galaxies* represents—and, more importantly, *explains*—Malzberg's eventual failure to discover a tolerable compromise. For this reason, if for no other, it is a superb piece of work. It is not so much a book of the science fiction mythos as a book *about* that mythos, seeking to discover both its nature and its functions. Its exploration is conducted in a thoroughly practical manner: in the writing of a science fiction story together with a commentary upon that story, revealing not only *what* is being done but *why*. There has been a glut of works about science fiction in the last decade, with fans, critics, and writers all trying to get in on the act, but there is no book which provides a better account of the nature of SF and the forces limiting its potential as an art-form than *Galaxies*. It is a classic of the *genre*.

Let us digress, for a while, in order to consider more deeply the matter of *competition*. Robert A. Heinlein is reputed to have remarked at one time that science fiction writers are competing for the public's beer money and must conduct themselves accordingly. Stanislaw Lem, who comes from a culture in which the capitalist ethic is not so strongly entrenched, reacted with understandable horror to this statement. He replied—realistically—that if this were so then science fiction had no chance, and the brewers would always win in a canter.

The notion of competition between writers is nonsensical so far as artistic considerations are concerned. The competition between writers in the marketplace of readership is a product of the economic assumptions pertaining to the philosophy of mass-production.

The U.S.A., *alma mater* of mass-production, first expanded industrial methods to include the production of fiction in the late nineteenth century with the emergence of the dime novel. Since then,

American mass-produced literature has passed through three principal stages: the pulp magazine, the comic book, and the paperback. Fiction produced specifically for these media has been shaped almost entirely by the economic forces pertaining to its marketing. Like all mass-produced fare, the product has to be made quickly, easily, and cheaply, and it has to appeal to the greatest possible number of potential consumers.

Once the basic product was established, however, producers had to compete with one another. This was done by advertising, and particularly that aspect of advertising known as "brand warfare." With the aid of vigorous "natural selection," the publishers of dime novels and pulp magazines carved up the audience by creating *brands* of pulp fiction (the western, the detective story, science fiction, *et al.*) to sort out the various kinds of demand at large in the mass audience. Companies do the same thing today when they devise advertising pitches for dog foods, washing powders, and brands of beer. Mass-produced fiction, however, always had one advantage over most consumer goods in that the fiction was both ad *and* product, at one and the same time.

Ads play upon certain psychological tendencies to anxiety. The ad, ideally, creates an anxiety that the product will dispel. The actual effects and nature of the product may have very little to do with the psychological pitch used to sell it—this is especially true of deodorants, cigarettes, and other poisons. Mass-produced fiction is designed simultaneously to *create* tension (usually under the *alias* of "suspense") and to relieve it. This function is clearly revealed by scrutiny of the criteria for story analysis which used to be employed by the Scott Meredith literary agency to evaluate work for mass-sales potential. The criteria were: 1. a sympathetic and believable *lead character*; 2. an urgent and vital *problem*; 3. complications caused the lead character's unsuccessful attempts to solve the problem; 4. the *crisis*; 5. the *resolution* in which the lead character solves the problem by means of his own courage and resourcefulness. (Try evaluating television commercials according to these criteria.)

When Malzberg referred to science fiction as "a sub-genre of romantic fiction," he was talking about science fiction as a brand of mass-produced fiction: science fiction created and shaped by publishers whose sole priority was consumer gratification. The rise of mass-produced fiction over the last hundred years has created problems for all writers who have embraced some artistic and aesthetic priorities of their own, in that their financial survival has very largely been tied up with their willingness also to meet the consumer gratification priority. In order to survive, it may not be necessary for a writer to compete against bottled beer, but it is certainly necessary for him to compete, if he wants to work in the SF field, with *The Rammers of Arcturus*. Indeed, this necessity applies rather more to the SF field than to any other, in that science fiction was the only *genre* born into, and for a long time largely confined within, the media of mass-produced fiction. Malzberg, together with perhaps a dozen other writers, has been engaged in the task of trying to utilize the vocabulary of ideas built up by the science fiction community for specific artistic and aesthetic ends. He has found it to be a thankless task, and being a man who knows the ins and outs of a racetrack, he is aware of the perils of investing heavily against the odds. These are the circumstances which have governed his career.

Malzberg's stories have lead characters who are none-too-strong, and he presents them, usually, with a relative lack of sympathy. This is in conscious opposition to the requirements of mass-produced fiction and the mythology of SF. They have problems, and their problems are, by and large, anxieties created by the lives they are living and the worlds they are living in. But these anxieties are not to be conveniently whisked away by the ad/product consumption ritual, for they are not artificial worries drummed up from tiny Freudian knots of repressed guilt, but real, deep-seated worries that arise from the structure of life itself. They do not yield to the placebo effect.

Malzberg's characters often feel that their problems *ought* to yield. They are often resentful when their problems *don't* yield. Usually, they complain a lot. They tend to be as frustrated as dogs escaped from Pavlov's laboratory who find their carefully inculcated pattern of conditioned reflexes woefully inadequate to cope with the real world. Malzberg's characters sometimes *think* that they live in fictions structured to the assumptions of advertising mythology, but they don't.

George Mercer, in *Day of the Burning*, is a bumbling cog in the bureaucratic machine of the New York City Welfare Department. He has twelve hours to prepare a case for the admission of Earth to the Galactic Federation. He can't. Unlike the hero of a Heinlein juvenile, he finds that his impassioned plea on behalf of mankind doesn't come ready-scripted with a built-in guarantee of success.

David, hero of *Tactics of Conquest,* has been selected to represent Good in a chess match against Evil, refereed by the Galactic Overlords. At least, he *thinks* he is Good and his opponent Evil, but it could, of course, be the other way round. Can he win? If so, should he? Will the referee put up with a draw? There is no way to find answers to the questions, or even to find out whether the questions are meaningful.

Harold Evans, in *Beyond Apollo*, has come back from the first mission to Venus with his companion dead and no explanation for the failure of the mission—or, rather, with an infinite number of equally viable or inviable explanations: humorous, dramatic, tragic, absurd, or just plain stupid. His superiors *demand* an explanation, a motivational account, but there seems to be no way for him to fit the event into their rational framework of expectations. It just doesn't *belong* there.

One can, of course, appreciate the mess that these characters are in. If I were stuck in circumstances such as these I'd be inclined to believe that I was stuck inside a science fiction story, and thus entitled to make use of the customary formularistic means of getting out of them. But that's just the point—in the absurd real world, as in these absurd fantasies, there *is* no means of getting out. Even the hero of *Underlay*, who is not involved with deep space or Galactic Overlords, but is simply commissioned by The Syndicate to exhume a body buried under the backstretch of Aqueduct racetrack because it is upsetting their form figures, can't help feeling that there is something surreally ridiculous about it all. Perhaps it's the time bomb implanted in his thigh—but it's more likely the crazy way in which the world works.

None of Malzberg's heroes ever find, when it comes to the crunch, that a new brand of deodorant *(deus ex machina* for *men)* will come to their rescue. They are stuck. And, as the hero of *Underlay* discovers as he is apprehended by Pinkertons in the act of desecrating the sacred turf, there isn't even any way of explaining.

The simple inapplicability of the science fictional mythos to real circumstances in the real world is demonstrated best of all by the case of Jonathan Herovit, science fiction writer. Herovit's problems, brought about by the extreme difficulties of trying to make a living—and, indeed, trying to exist at all—are quite insoluble. Not only can't Herovit make any headway, but neither can Kirk Poland, his tough, SF-writing *persona*. In the end, even Mack Miller, the all-conquering hero of the immortal endless series of Colonial Survey stories, finds that the real alien world of New York is far too tough to yield to his methods.

This, then, is the gospel according to Malzberg.

But is he cheating? Is he cheating the fans, cheating the sacred spirit of SF itself? Is it *fair* for a writer to introduce Galactic Overlords, spaceships, the future and alien planets into his stories without the attendant Asimovian aces-in-the-hole to bale out the lead character (be he ever so humble) when his unholy mess reaches a climax? Why, if Malzberg has such a low opinion of the SF mythos, doesn't he simply leave it alone?

Well, simply stated, because of exactly what he said in the introduction to *Final War and Other Fantasies*, because "it can be truly said that 98% of the available material and implications (of SF) which could concern a writer have not been touched." In that, he was right—and he will continue to be right as long as SF is marketed to perform the mythological function which it does perform.

Malzberg uses the symbolic vocabulary of SF in a manner strategically different from that in which the mass-producers employ it. He is not alone in this—J. G. Ballard and the writer who used to try and get out of Philip José Farmer were perhaps the pioneers of the direction of approach Malzberg adopts. Malzberg's subject matter has always been the alienated individual, and he has used the ideative vocabulary of SF to dramatize metaphorically the forces of alienation. The psychological *milieu* of all Malzberg's novels is the present—contemporary America. The manifest action is cast forward in time or sideways into an alien situation only in order to use the imaginative capital of SF. Malzberg has not tried to add to that mythos but has plundered it for his own uses. (One might wish that all SF writers were as apt at using it as they are at inventing it, but it is not so. We live in an age of specialization, and must accept its limitations.)

Perhaps the best way to analyze Malzberg's SF is to investigate the ways in which it grows out of the themes of those novels which are not SF.

Screen is about a man whose sex life consists of fantasized sexual congress with images projected on to a cinema screen. A sexual experiment with a real woman has no chance, because there is no way the reality can compete with the machine-assisted fantasy. At the end of the book, the hero takes the girl to the movies, offering her the chance to forsake cruel reality in favor of the preferable fantasy. "You're just afraid," he tells her. "You're just afraid to be in the movies. You're afraid because you might find out that they're better than the life you're leading and you wouldn't be able to stand it. That's all. Why don't you give it a chance?" She can't—but that doesn't matter. He can—he has adapted to the technological environment with its commercially-produced impossible dreams in the supremely logical manner.

Screen is perhaps the most optimistic of *all* of Malzberg's novels, for though it offers no solution, it does offer hope in capitulation, in adaptation. *Screen* is not science fiction, but is incipiently so in that it recognizes the role played by the technological media in modern life and is a speculation about ways of adjustment to that role. If it were a science fiction story, it would be essentially no different, but would push the man/machine relationship to some kind of logical extreme. This happens in the short story Malzberg contributed to the anthology he co-edited with Edward Ferman, *Final Stage.* In the same way *Screen* is "ancestral" to many of Malzberg's later novels dealing with adaptation (or the failure to adapt) to "false" technological environments: *The Falling Astronauts, Beyond Apollo,* etc. In these stories it becomes impossible for characters to construct coherent motivational accounts for actions carried out in technologically dehumanized circumstances.

In another non-SF novel, *Underlay,* the focus is another class of alienating forces: the arbitrary workings of chance which still haunt those areas of experience we try to make rational and predictable. The horseplayer is constantly faced with the problem of picking the winner—a problem which seems to be amenable to a rational and methodical approach, provided that a large enough range of variables is studied and weighed according to significance. There are innumerable sets of procedural rules which might be drawn up to increase the punter's chances of selecting winners. The vast majority, however, don't work. *Underlay* is concerned with people trying desperately to come to terms with the random element of life—the element which threatens to render life irrational and meaningless. The racetrack is the microcosm in which they work. In another book, *Overlay*, these random forces, invested by virtue of their unpredictability with a kind of menace, become a race of aliens plotting the destruction of Earth. There is no escape, whether the symbol of the Galactic Overlords is invoked or not. The odds, as every punter knows, are loaded.

Even when the rules of the game are much more firmly fixed, as in the chess tournament of *Tactics of Conquest*, there is no escape. Someone wins, someone loses, but the *meaning* of the winning and losing remains unknown; the Galactic Overlords and their purpose are quite enigmatic. Mercer, in *Day of the Burning*, is also playing with fixed rules—the regulations of the Welfare Department covering his dealings with clients—but he too is helpless, in that the rules have no relevance to reality, are designed to operate in circumstances which do not exist, and are quite useless for the vital business of negotiating with the threatening aliens.

This kind of *anomie*—a normlessness brought about by the absence or inappropriateness of rules to regulate action and thought—is at the core of both Malzberg's most desperate fictions (*Galaxies*, "Final War," *The Gamesman*) and his most absurd (the K. M. O'Donnell novels *Dwellers of the Deep* and *Gather in the Hall of the Planets*). It is here, by an inevitable analogy, that the situation of the aspiring SF writer is thrust into his stories, as character as well as creator. The writer who attempts to use the SF mythos as Malzberg has is bedevilled by the inappropriateness of the "rules" pertaining to the production and consumption of mass-produced fiction.

In these ways, fiction which represents the alienation of the individual using the microcosms of the cinema, the racetrack, the writer's battle with his typewriter, extends naturally by strategic exaggeration into fiction which invokes macrocosmic symbols: aliens, futures, black galaxies.

There has been, of course, no possibility of a solution for Malzberg as an SF writer. He has decided to stop being one—at least in the way he represents himself to himself, and to his audience. Perhaps he will stop writing altogether. Retiring from the fray is, of course, a compromise rather than a solution, and whether it proves a satisfactory compromise, so far as Malzberg is concerned, remains to be seen. Perhaps, though, the career of a writer who specializes in frustration can make no sense unless it can come itself to such a totally frustrating close.

POSTSCRIPT (1979)

Since this essay was written in 1976 Barry Malzberg has published several SF short stories and one SF novel. The novel—*Chorale*—is one of his best works. This does not entirely undermine the point made in the conclusion of the essay as it stands—Malzberg has declared that he is merely "keeping his hand in" and that he has not reversed his decision to quit. As a commentary on that decision as it was taken in 1975 the above piece remains pertinent. If Malzberg were to return to full-time SF writing, or even to recover a fraction of the commitment to the *genre* which he had in 1968-74, he would probably find the recovered situation just as frustrating as it was then, for the same reasons.

Some critics have been inclined to see Malzberg's retirement as evidence of arbitrary paranoia rather than a symptom of the ambiguous historical situation of the *genre*. He is not, however, the only writer to have reacted angrily against the impositions placed upon him by those expecting him to conform to conventions of *genre* SF writing which have more to do with the marketplace than with literary potential. Harlan Ellison, Robert Silverberg, and Kurt Vonnegut, in explaining their own reactions against the label, echo the sentiments expressed in *Herovit's World* (and, indeed, to some extent the book echoes *them*). The literary marketplace is, however, a fast-changing arena, and there may soon come a time when even Malzberg may feel happier about the situation than he does now. *Chorale* may be the first crack in the dam of frustration, and the dam may eventually be weakened enough to burst. I hope so.

IV.

THE METAMORPHOSIS
OF ROBERT SILVERBERG

Robert Silverberg has been the most prolific science fiction writer of the past two decades. A bibliography published in *The Magazine of Fantasy & Science Fiction* in April 1974 credits him with more than sixty SF books published between 1955 and 1972. It also credits him with more than sixty nonfiction books, more than two hundred uncollected short stories, and with the editorship of some twenty-odd anthologies. There remains a great deal of work which did not fall within the scope of the bibliography, and Silverberg's total published wordage between those years ran into the tens of millions. He was, in April 1974, not yet forty years old.

Silverberg's productivity is without parallel, but no less phenomenal has been the dramatic change which has overtaken his writing in the last ten years.

He began his writing career in the SF field in 1954, selling a juvenile SF book *Revolt on Alpha C* and the short story "Gorgon Planet" to the British magazine *Nebula*. He was astonishingly prolific in the years 1956-58, but in 1959 he virtually abandoned the shrinking SF market in favor of a host of others which, between them, could keep up with his productivity. In the next seven years a handful of SF novels appeared, but these were mostly derived from old material. In the late sixties he began again to regard SF as one of his primary working media (the other being nonfiction of high quality), but the Silverberg who thus returned to the field was by no means the Silverberg who had left it.

His work—and his own attitude to his work—had undergone a considerable change. An account of the metamorphosis in personal terms was published in *Foundation* no. 7/8 (March, 1975), and in the collection of autobiographical essays by SF writers, *Hell's Cartographers*, edited by Brian Aldiss and Harry Harrison and published by Weidenfeld and Nicolson. What follows is an account of the evolution of the work.

The bulk of Silverberg's early work was written very easily, and reads very easily. Most of his early short stories are puzzle-stories in which people become involved with unlikely situations (usually featuring unlikely aliens) and obtain a resolution with an altogether-too-likely clever twist. Many other writers were producing similar stories—Robert Sheckley, perhaps, being the most adept with the type. Like Sheckley, Silverberg specialized in a casual irony, but while Sheckley's man-alien encounters always tended to be comical, and in later years became outrightly farcical, Silverberg retained a slightly darker shade of comedy. When the turnaround came and the biters were bitten, they were bitten good and hard.

In one of the most frequently reprinted stories of the period, "Absolutely Inflexible," the protagonist is the man with the job of condemning all arriving time-travellers to the moon to protect a disease-free Earth from possible infection. Inevitably, he begins to tinker with a confiscated time machine, and winds up looking at himself from the wrong side of the desk. In other similarly-patterned stories, there is a distinct bitterness which undermines the calculated triviality of the form. In "Eve and the 23 Adams," a starship captain is tricked by a girl who signs on as "crew girl" under false pretenses, only wanting a free ride to a colony in space. The captain tricks her into fulfilling her function unawares, but finds when the ship reaches its destination that she is his son's intended bride. In "Warm Man," an empathic "leech" is sustained by the emotional troubles of his neighbors—until he encounters a small boy who has more troubles than he can take, and the power to broadcast them powerfully.

Characters in gimmick-stories do not always fall victim to their own failings—sometimes they are simply fall guys too innocent to know that the universe will always cheat them. Silverberg wrote "Schlemihl stories" of this variety too, but again he frequently found the darker aspect of the fatalistic conviction. In "Ozymandias," archeologists working on an alien world, trying to make sense of the ruins of a once-great civilization, find a robot who can tell them all they want to know. But he can also inform the military wing of the expedition concerning the weapons with which the civilization destroyed itself. The presentation here is somber—written in the shadow of the H-bomb, its irony was by no means comic. In the same year (1958), Silverberg published "Road to Nightfall," perhaps the most impressive of his earliest stories (it had been written several years before), but quite atypical of his mass-produced fiction. It describes social decay in a city whose food supplies are cut off in the aftermath of a war. Its ruthless conviction stands in contrast not only to the triviality of Silverberg's other work, but also to the committed triviality of the market to which the mass-produced stories were slanted. The demands of the market were that ingenuity should triumph, whether it was the ingenuity of the author in designed stories like mousetraps whose final brutal *snap* could be excused by the principle of poetic justice, or the ingenuity of a character in cancelling problems one against another and averting disaster by a slick, superficial cleverness making light of any sober implications a story might contain.

The early Silverberg was an intelligent writer with an active mind, and he could produce a good line in slick, superficial cleverness. A good example is the novel *Master of Life and Death*, where the central character is faced with a quickfire sequence of problems which sustain him in furious action as he first juggles with them, and finally, with brilliant sleight-of-hand, makes them all disappear. World and hero alike tremble on disaster throughout: the Earth has a population problem, the protagonist is bending the rules, aliens are interfering with the space program, and someone has invented an immortality serum which can only make things worse. The author's hand, however, is incomparably quicker than the eye, and the problems disappear.

Such conjuring tricks supplied Silverberg's best early work with readability and interest, but as his productivity increased he came to rely more and more on the routines of pulp cliché, in which heroes are moved through a potentially infinite series of standard scenarios until a *deus ex machina* can be evoked to tidy things up. Many space operas, often produced under pseudonyms (*Starhaven* as Ivar Jorgenson, *Aliens from Space* as David Osborne, *The Plot Against Earth* as Calvin M. Knox, etc.) follow this pattern.

Two novels, *Recalled to Life* and *Invaders from Earth*, raised issues deserving more serious consideration (the possibility of medical revivification of the dead, and the manner in which advertising methods may be used to manipulate public opinion), and did not skip so lightly over their implications. Science fiction provides—at least potentially— a dramatic framework within which hypothetical questions of this nature may be effectively explored, and the headlong gallop of social and scientific progress which carries us all apace into the future makes it necessary that such questions *ought* to be explored in whatever frameworks are available. In *Recalled to Life* especially, Silverberg showed a degree of insight rare among his contemporaries, and this remains the most interesting of his early novels; but in both books the plot acts in opposition to the theme. *Recalled to Life*, like *Master of Life and Death*, moves too quickly to a conjuring trick dénouement whose neatness trivializes its impact, while *Invaders from Earth* relies heavily on the methodology of pulp melodrama.

The books are exciting, they involve the reader. Will our hero, by submitting voluntarily to death and revivication, get the good publicity required to make resurrection acceptable to the people? Will our hero, having put the public in the right frame of mind to accept the genocide of the Ganymede aliens, manage to thwart the villains and save them after all? The questions are set up so as to tug at the puppet-strings of the reader, but the trouble is that such tugging works because it conforms to a tried and tested pattern. There is little room for deviation or for innovation, and the competent writer is trapped by his own professionalism. When the first period of Silverberg's work in the SF field came to an end in 1958, it could not be said that he was anything more than competent. He had been voted a Hugo in 1956 as the "most promising new writer," but had hardly begun to fulfill that promise.

Outside science fiction, in the *genre* wilderness where Silverberg produced anything and everything for seven years, he was able to exploit his casual extravagance to the full. The problem of developing hypothetical questions did not arise, and there was just as little scope for innovation in the content of the work as there was in the method.

Of the science fiction novels which appeared during the years 1959-66, some were inflated short stories and others pure hackwork. One or two (*Collision Course* and *Seed of Earth* especially) were earnest in their confrontation of central issues, but fell conspicuously between two stools: they lacked the pace and neatness of the best early novels, but had not enough real depth to compensate. Several short stories, however—and especially two published in 1963—were exceptional.

"The Pain Peddlers" is a "biter bit" story whose construction is reminiscent of the early work, but with a particularly harsh bitterness hitherto unrevealed.

An executive for the media has the job of persuading people in need of costly operations to forego anesthetic so that their pain can be broadcast to a sensation-hungry public. One such operation—a colossal success from his point of view, though the patient dies—leads to his being attacked by the victim's son, and injured so badly that he himself needs an operation. The rest follows logically.

The story has less in common with the straightforward twist-of-fate in "Absolutely Inflexible" than with the cruel irony of "Warm Man." The warm man fed on the troubles of others, but was destroyed because the world had far more trouble than he could handle. In "The Pain Peddlers," it is the multitude who feed on trouble, and it is their *demand* which puts too much pressure on the supply. In this kind of perspective reverse there is a clue to the nature of the change which was overtaking Silverberg's writing.

The second story, "To See the Invisible Man," was the best piece Silverberg had produced to date. Its protagonist is punished for repeated transgressions of the law by expulsion from society: he is declared "invisible." The condition, he finds, has both advantages and disadvantages: he can steal or play the *voyeur* without interference, but he cannot get medical help and is cut off from all human intercourse. In a sense, he is godlike in his ability to interfere mischievously in the ordered lives of others, but he is also totally vulnerable—if he goes too far, "accidents" may happen. In the end, it is the torment of being unable to communicate which triumphs over all other aspects of the situation, and his torture is complete when even another invisible man refuses to recognize him. When his sentence ends, he is approached by that same invisible man, who has by now learned what *he* had learned, and who now pleads for recognition. After an agonized moment of decision, he embraces the man, and goes to trial facing probable condemnation for a second time.

The situation at the end of "To See the Invisible Man" permits the invocation of the same irony so characteristic of Silverberg's early work, but it is rejected. The theme destroys the method, and the actual meaning of what is happening in the story forbids its trivialization. The mousetrap is unsprung; the invisible man does not turn away to confirm the neatness of situation and system, and the implications of the central idea are left naked. Silverberg shows himself to be more interested in the problems of the character than those of the storyteller.

The role of the protagonist in Silverberg's fiction after 1963 is generally different from the roles characteristic of his early work. In the early work, the protagonist is usually either a Schlemihl, falling victim to the story's hidden trap, or a hero, whose task is to conjure solutions out of its problematic debris. After 1963, the heroes are often victims, and the victims are often heroes.

A good example of the new ambivalence may be found in the short story "Halfway House" (1966), in which the obvious ironic superficiality is again subverted. A man suffering from terminal cancer is called upon to justify his claim to prolonged life before he is allowed to use an alien transport system to visit a world where his illness can be cured. The price asked from him is five years service in the transport network—and he finds himself assigned to the Halfway House as the selector who must decide on other men's claims to justify their use of the system. Like the invisible man, he finds himself in a quasi-godlike situation (a master of life and death), but finds the exercise of power an intolerable burden on his conscience. He is not given the opportunity to juggle a host of problems and cancel them with superficial logical neatness, as was the protagonist of the early novel, but must simply live with the sympathy he feels for other men and their troubles.

By 1965 Silverberg was in the process of changing his writing philosophy. His production was cut and he began devoting a great deal of attention to certain particular works—to nonfiction books which were impressive works of scholarship (*The Great Wall of China* and *The Golden Dream*) and to some of his science fiction.

He found it impossible to maintain a punishing work schedule and simultaneously devote a great deal of thought to his work, and fell ill as a result of driving himself too hard. With the brake on, however, he began to fulfill his real potential. He produced the series of stories making up the book *To Open the Sky*, in which the architects of a religious movement use the power of faith to manipulate human history, instituting genetic selection for mental powers, and staging a messianic rebirth as a prelude to the metaphorical rebirth of mankind in achieving interstellar travel. He also produced *The Time Hoppers*, in which he built one of his earliest idea stories ("Hopper") into a craftsmanlike novel. His major work of the period, however, consisted of two new novels of startling quality: *Thorns* and *Hawksbill Station* (also called *The Anvil of Time*). All of these books—and several others—were published in 1967.

Thorns follows up the subject matter of "The Pain Peddlers," but builds around an emotional core which has much in common with "To See the Invisible Man." Duncan Chalk is the pain peddler who feeds himself and markets for the world the suffering of his chosen victims. The two victims of the novel are Minner Burris and Lona Kelvin, two people forced by circumstance into states of extreme alienation, who are brought together by Chalk for a brief and tragic love affair. Burris has been stripped of his humanity by alien beings who have *literally* alienated him by surgery. It is also in the literal sense that Lona has been *stripped* of something essential to her identity, in that ova removed from her body have been used in a massive experiment in test-tube breeding. In conclusion, their love transcends the script which Chalk provides, and they destroy the vampiric being, hitting back *through* him at the world which oppresses them. ("They want to devour us," says Burris at one point. "They want to put us in the freak show." *They* is everybody.) Though love triumphs over evil, it is not the happiness of the ending which is remarkable, but its fierceness. *Thorns* is an emotionally violent book. No pulp clichés move its plot, and there is no elegant sleight-of-mind about the revolution. The concern of the novel, mechanically as well as thematically, is the predicament of its hero-victims, in elaborating, exaggerating, and analyzing the quality of their alienaton.

Hawksbill Station, by contrast, is a book drained of all emotional drama. It is neither elaborate nor exaggerated, but its analysis of the state of alienation which is established for the characters by the hypothetical situation cuts much deeper. The station is a place of exile for political dissidents expelled from a near-future U.S.A. It is located in the late Cambrian Period, and so far as its occupants are aware there is no question of return. Barrett, "king" of the station, is tortured by a physical injury and by the memory of his betrayal. One prisoner is building a woman out of rags and fragments of Cambrian crustacea, and another is conducting experiments in psychical research, trying to escape by breaking through to a higher level of consciousness, transcending time and the Hawksbill equations which make their exile absolute. When a new arrival in the camp begins writing reports on the possibility of rehabilitating the inmates, there is no way for the others to know whether he is reacting to his circumstances by manufacturing a convenient illusion (as they are) or whether a real possibility of release now exists. So far as Barrett is personally concerned, in fact, the question of release no longer seems important—but there is a wider context in which the ultimate prison might thus be transformed into the first outpost beyond a gateway to infinity.

These novels belonged to an entirely new species so far as Silverberg's work was concerned. Science fiction, by its very nature, is the perfect medium for pulp romance: its vocabulary of ideas provides limitless possibilites for adventurous confrontation and the resolution of conventionally impossible situations by conventionally impossible means. By the same token, it provides the natural medium for the hypothetical exploration of real possibilities. In his earlier career, Silverberg had written both kinds, his mass-produced hackwork exploiting the former market while *Recalled to Life*, "Road to Nightfall," etc. belonged to the second category. Both these exercises are primarily concerned with the mechanics of plotting, and characterization is secondary—indeed, often neglected altogether.

But science fiction can also be used in a different way: as a means of imaginatively exploring situations which are exaggerated versions of actual states of being. In this case the vocabulary of ideas becomes not a reservoir of commercial fantasies or a construction kit for imaginative hypotheses, but a repertoire of metaphors. (To draw a simple analogy in order to make this clear, Aesop's fables use animal stereotypes as a vocabulary of metaphors. The fables are not fantasies, nor are they explorations of real possibility—they present general principles applicable to real situations in dramatic guise. The fables are, of course, admonitory, but a vocabulary of metaphors may also be used analytically, not to tell people what to do in certain situations, but to try and define by analogy exactly what is happening.)

In "To See the Invisible Man," *Thorns*, and *Hawksbill Station* Silverberg uses science fictional ideas to dramatize situations of extreme alienation. What is present in the real world as a feeling (the sensation of being remote from other people, the concept of essential humanity being eroded by the impersonality of modern living, the paradox of the self's omnipotence within the universe of the mind and its sometimes-horrifying vulnerability in the universe at large) is realized in these stories. The invisible man *is* remote from his fellows, omnipotent and yet vulnerable. Burris *is* an alien being; Lona Kelvin *has* been robbed of something essential by a world in which she has become the remainder of a socioscientific experiment. Barrett *is* required to survive in an environment depleted of virtually all human contact and meaning. These exercises are not primarily concerned with the mechanics of plotting but with the human predicament, and characterization becomes all-important.

The same characters recur in Silverberg's work of the following year. Sometimes the state of alienation is given different ideative guise, sometimes the same device is used again. In "Flies," Silverberg's contribution to *Dangerous Visions*, and in the novel *The Man in The Maze*, Minner Burris, with slight amendment to the manner of his alteration by the aliens, crops up again under different names. The first story has the familiar ironic twist, but with the new agony instead of the old dry humor, while in the second the central character compounds his alienation by retiring to the center of a great maze where he is unreachable as well as intolerable. Silverberg looked at the question in many ways, and explored many possible resolutions. In *Thorns* the traditional answer—love—is put forward for consideration, while in *Hawksbill Station* and *The Man in the Maze* there are more rational, if less hopeful, reconciliations. In "Flies" there is no answer—the victim is irrevocably trapped. And so it is in "Passengers," a Nebula Award-winning short story in which people are the helpless victims of periodic infestations by aliens who take over and use their bodies as they please.

To the same period belong *To Live Again* and *The Masks of Time* (aka *Vornan-19*)—two novels which are hypothetical in character rather than metaphorical. The former is strongly plotted, and has a theme reminiscent of *Recalled to Life*, featuring a world in which mind-tapes provide the means for the dead to be resurrected as parasites upon the living. That this theme is closely allied to Silverberg's new universe of discourse is evident in the fact that the idea of putting two minds in one skull was used to dramatize the alienated condition in a later novel, *The Second Trip*. *The Masks of Time* is, by contrast, all-but-devoid of plot. It is a curious novel describing the activities of a time-tourist who comes to observe the apocalyptic climax to the twentieth century and becomes a part of it in a quasi-messianic fashion. The strategy of using a "man of the future" as an "objective" observer to provide a commentary on our own time is about as classical a method as science fiction boasts (*e.g.*, Grant Allen's *The British Barbarians*, John Beresford's *The Hampdenshire Wonder*, Olaf Stapledon's *Odd John*, etc.), but Silverberg uses it not as a vehicle for social comment and criticism but as a symbol of rebirth. The time traveller refers back to a "Time of Sweeping," which makes it clear that our world is doomed, but he attempts to infect the world with his own Utopian vision, and he is himself the incarnate proof of human regeneration. This book is particularly significant in that the myth of rebirth and regeneration is one which has natural links to the problems of alienation—and the forging of that link was to become the predominant concern of Silverberg's subsequent work.

Despite his illness in 1966 Silverberg was still producing books at a phenomenal rate in 1967. In February of 1968, however, he was interrupted by disaster when his house burned down, destroying almost the whole apparatus of his life. It was rebuilt, but Silverberg was led to write in his autobiographical essay that: "I was never the same again. Until the night of the fire I had never...been touched by the real anguish of life.... The fire and certain other dark events some months earlier had marked an end to my apparent immunity to life's pain, and drained from me, evidently forever, much of the bizarre energy that had allowed me to write a dozen or more books of high quality in a single year."

He began again. For a novella collection on the theme of man's vulnerability to technological disaster he wrote "How It Was When the Past Went Away," about an epidemic amnesia which forces a city's inhabitants to start their lives all over. He also produced the novella "Nightwings"—a nostalgic, almost lyrical return to the exotic backgrounds of his old *Science Fiction Adventures* space operas, but with a sober plot which was transformed in two sequels, "Perris Way" and "To Jorslem," first into a study of alienation and finally into a myth of rebirth. A Watcher, whose task it is to warn Earth of alien invasion, cannot rouse effective opposition when it comes. The aliens take over Earth, and he becomes a stranger in the world they are beginning to change. Ultimately, however, the invasion paves the way for a human renaissance, and the Watcher undergoes transcendental metamorphosis into a quasi-angelic being.

It was also shortly after the fire that he wrote the superb short story "Sundance," in which the morality of colonialism and the possibilities inherent in human contact with alien beings are explored in a compact and elegant piece of prose where coexistent alternative realities show the issue from several perspectives. The same question became the starting point for the novel *Downward to the Earth*, a *tour-de-force* which brought together many of the threads of his past work. Its hero, Gundersen, returns to the planet Belzagor with the idea of atoning in some way for the cruelties which he was once party to imposing upon the natives, who were then enslaved but have since been recognized as "people." One particular crime which haunts him is the fact that he once prevented seven of the aliens from going to the ritual rebirth which forms the core of their religion and their life. He ultimately follows the path to rebirth himself, cursed by one of the seven and aided by another, to become a new kind of being, at once human *and* alien. Symbolically, at least, this was the most satisfactory resolution to the problems with which Silverberg was now concerned that he ever achieved. It is, however, not too difficult to design surreal and symbolic solutions to real problems.

The motif of transcendental transfiguration as an "answer" to the pain implicit in the human condition is, of course, central to most forms of religious belief—and in particular to the Christian doctrine of personal salvation. The influence of Christian mythos is evident in such books as *The Masks of Time* and *Nightwings*, but in the novel which followed *Downward to the Earth*, *Tower of Glass*, it becomes overt. The novel draws a parallel between Simeon Krug, who is trying to make contact with the infinite universe beyond Earth *via* a great tower intended to beam and receive messages to and from other worlds, and Thor Watchman, an android to whom Krug himself (the creator of the androids) is both deity and hope of salvation. When Krug discovers the secret religion of the androids, with himself as its godhead, he tells Watchman that in his eyes androids are mere things—products unworthy of any special consideration—and devastates Watchman's hopes. The android retaliates by destroying the tower, and condemning Krug's analogous hopes.

The surreal novel *Son of Man* was a logical outgrowth of this climate of thought. The world in which the book is set is not the physical planet Earth but the Earth of human perception—the model world of the mind. It takes place not in a future of extrapolated possibility but a future of psychological potential. Sensations are incarnated as landscape—there are places called *Old*, *Heavy*, and *Slow*. Modes of psychological orientation become alternative human species: *skimmers*, *awaiters*, *destroyers*. The protagonist watches the ceremony of the Five Rites, culminating in the Shaping of the Sky, but his presence upsets the progress of the rites and he is referred by a being called Wrong to the Well of First Things, where he is called upon to forsake his alienated isolation and accept the whole burden of humanity. Here, the author has abandoned even his metaphorical structures, and is experimenting with pure symbology.

In two novels which followed *Son of Man* Silverberg developed a new direction of approach to his central concern. *The World Inside* and *A Time of Changes* focus not on the state of alienation but on the kind of circumstances which generate alienation. The first deals with an overpopulated world whose citizens are gathered into superskyscraper Urbmons, forced to live in such close association with one another that social relationships disintegrate under the strain. The second deals with an alien society in which communication—especially emotional communication—is a sin. One may regard *The World Inside* as a metaphorical exaggeration of modern city life, and *A Time of Changes* as a metaphorical exaggeration of contemporary social convention, but there are no symbolic transcendental solutions here. From the World Inside there is no escape at all, while the hero of *A Time of Changes* clings desperately but hopelessly to the traditional solution that love can triumph over any adversity.

This particular aspect of Silverberg's work culminated in a return to quasi-mysticism in the novel *The Book of Skulls*, in which four characters are weighed and minutely examined in terms of their formation by and their relationship with the environment. The metaphor is stripped from the situation—the world of the book is contemporary America—but is retained in the goal which is described so as to provide a "set of rules" for the interaction of the characters one with another. There is a promise that the "winners" in the game may achieve a certain immortality, but only on special terms.

While *The Book of Skulls* summed up Silverberg's study of the forces causing alienation, *Dying Inside* summed up his extensive exploration of the state of alienation. Again, the imaginative component is stripped down to a single definitive metaphor. The world of the book remains contemporary America, but the protagonist, David Selig, is a receptive telepath. His talent gives him godlike powers of perception and understanding, but he remains ultimately vulnerable in the face of what he perceives and understands. The central paradox of the problem of alienation is hardly capable of more elegant dramatization. Within the book we are offered the predicament of Kafka's heroes as a standard for comparison, but it has much closer parallels with Sartre's *Nausea*. The plot of the novel is consummately simple: Selig is losing his talent, losing his ability to understand his fellow men and in so doing becoming like them, losing his alienness. The central issue is starkly clear: is it a case of heads they win, tails he loses? Can the "death" of his present self, his "metamorphosis," really provide a "rebirth" into the human world?

The Book of Skulls and *Dying Inside* completed a phase in Silverberg's career—together they constitute a kind of punctuation mark. In order to display the context in which this work may, in my opinion, be best understood, I have neglected mention of a number of other works also published between 1967 and 1972. Although this work is, for the most part, peripheral to the developing core of his work, it is not necessarily inferior. There are a number of other stories which construct situations which are metaphors of alienation—some of them, like the time-paradox novel *Up the Line* and the short stories "Caliban" and "The Reality Trip," are much lighter in treatment and recover a wryness usually associated with his older work. Others fit closely into the scheme I have mapped out but seem to be adjuncts to it—the brilliant novelette "In Entropy's Jaws" is thematically related to *Son of Man*, while *The Second Trip* forms a bridge between *To Live Again* and *Dying Inside*, following up the idea of two minds in one body while developing the idea of the receptive telepath as an archetype of the alienated man at a much more sophisticated level than "Warm Man." There still remain two good juvenile novels (*Gate of Worlds* and *Across a Billion Years*) and much more short work, including two more award winners ("Good News from the Vatican" and "The Feast of St. Dionysus").

Three major works published after *Dying Inside*, which extend the central pattern of Silverberg's work, are the novels *The Stochastic Man* and *Shadrach in the Furnace*, and the novella "Born with the Dead." The first work reverses the theme of *Dying Inside*, using the acquisition of an extra-sensory power as the means of alienation. It gives the impression of being a slightly demoralized work, taking as its major premise a deterministic fatalism which renders the precognitive protagonist impotent to exploit his talent. "Born with the Dead" is also fatalistic in its insistence that the hero cannot rearrange the order of things in order to fulfill his desires. The story finds a suitable resolution within the scope of its own premises, but it is one which is achieved in spite of the actions of the hero rather than through them. *Shadrach in the Furnace*, by contrast, hovers for a long time on the brink of fatalism before allowing its central character to strike a crucial blow for freedom—not only *his* freedom but seemingly for the very principle of free will, which had almost been relegated to negligibility in the worldview of the half-dozen preceding novels. The defiant existentialist gesture, however, proved to be the final twist in the plot of this phase of Silverberg's career. He abandoned science fiction writing for several years.

Silverberg's newest novel, *Lord Valentine's Castle*, has recently been published. No one (perhaps not even Silverberg) can tell whether it heralds the beginning of a new phase in the career of this remarkable writer. If it is to be· so, then it will presumably be a *new* phase, dedicated to different concerns, and another metamorphosis may be necessary if he is to find new creative energy. It would be astonishing if this were possible, but Silverberg's record is such that expecting the astonishing from him is no more than reasonable.

V.

UTOPIA—AND AFTERWARDS

SOCIOECONOMIC SPECULATION
IN THE SF OF MACK REYNOLDS

Isaac Asimov once expressed the opinion that science fiction changed direction during the 1940s, when a period in which its dominant concern was technological invention gave way to a period in which its dominant concern became the social effects of technological progress. There was, according to this argument, no radical change in content, but simply a trend towards "sociological" extrapolation. This observation is not altogether false, in that it recognizes the new editorial requirements introduced into the corner of the pulp magazine market occupied by SF magazines by John W. Campbell, but it nevertheless fails to draw attention to the fact that Hugo Gernsback originally considered "scientifiction" to be an implicitly Utopian species of literature, one of whose main functions was to herald a new technological Golden Age. What really happened in the forties—primarily in *Astounding Science Fiction*—was that writers began to cast a rather more critical eye upon the implications of technological advance, and lost their naive and optimistic faith in the Gernsbackian "Age of Power Freedom." There is, therefore, a sense in which even pulp science fiction has always been "sociological"—which is to say, interested in the future prospects of human societies. At the same time, however, science fiction writers have been almost unilaterally scornful of sociology itself— and the other social sciences also—apparently considering them to be inferior to the natural sciences and hardly deserving to be used as bases for extrapolative thought. No writer can produce an image of future society without speculating about the politics of future society and the economics of future society, yet there are very few *genre* writers who have ever felt the need to refer to political or economic science before embarking upon such speculation. In some cases this refusal has proved pernicious, in that we still come across images of future society based on such stupid and obsolete assumptions as those of crude social Darwinism; in other cases it has simply resulted in the unthinking translocation of present-day political and economic systems into the future (even into the far-flung futures of galactic civilizations). It is, perhaps,

49

a sad comment that the only conscious attempt in *genre* SF to use a *theory* of history to construct a future history for mankind is James Blish's *Cities in Flight* tetralogy, which borrows not from social science but from the metaphysical philosophy of history concocted by Oswald Spengler.

The reasons for this reluctance to use sociological theory are various. Partly, it is a simple failure of imagination. Partly, it reflects a genuinely unsatisfactory situation in modern sociology as regards theories of social change. Partly, however, it is due to the fact that science fiction as a popular *genre* is American in origin and inspiration, and that American social philosophy has always been allergic to discussions of theories of social change because it is difficult to begin such discussion without taking into account the most influential theory of social change, which is that of Karl Marx. Marxist social theory and Marxist political rhetoric (though there is no *necessary* logical connection between them) are so closely associated and interwoven that hostility to the latter inevitably engenders hostility to the former, and this hostility tends also to stifle discussion of subsequent contributions to the theory of social change which, even if they are opposed to Marxist thought, nevertheless have to take it into account. The political climate in America, which has conditioned this allergic response during the last half-century, is largely responsible for the awkward predicament of American sociology as well as the failure of American science fiction to pay any real attention to the possible contribution of social science to the art of speculative extrapolation.

One might imagine that the situation in Eastern Europe would be very different, in that the governmental systems of those countries openly espouse Marxist theories of society. Unfortunately, this is not the case, for here too the attitude to the political rhetoric of Marxism dominates and determines attitudes to the theory of social change. The "official" position of such governments is that social change has, in accordance with Marxist theory (though this claim is highly dubious), been brought to its appropriate conclusion, and that there is therefore no further scope for speculation about the changes which might overtake society in the future. Soviet SF, therefore, presents a consistent tone of optimistic self-congratulation while being utterly devoid of any serious socioeconomic speculation. The simple fact is that no political system is inclined to tolerate the thought of its own mortality, and that socioeconomic speculation in fiction or nonfiction is always likely to be construed as being subversive. In the West, such speculation is far from being completely stifled, but diplomacy makes much of it rather weak, and stimulates much activity in the realm of apologetics. In science fiction, which is a mass-market *genre,* diplomacy usually rules despite a persistent tendency to parodic iconoclasm. The fifties produced a great number of stories which commented, at least metaphorically, on issues of contemporary political concern, and this trend has continued to the present day; but what is involved is generally the expression of opinion on particular matters (civil rights, the space program, etc.) rather than attempts to analyze fundamental issues concerned with socioeconomic change. The number of stories which deal with post-capitalist society (however this is envisaged) is really very small, and few of those that do exist refer explicitly to any assumptions about mechanisms of social change.

There is, however, one American writer who has in recent years made it his special mission to speculate about the social and economic situations of the near future and their possible patterns of development. This is Mack Reynolds, whose family background appears to have equipped him with a thorough familiarity with Marxist thought (both political rhetoric and social theory), and also with a healthy scepticism regarding all manner of political and economic presuppositions. Reynolds is not a writer who has attracted attention on account of the aesthetic merits of his prose, but his unique situation within contemporary American science fiction nevertheless makes him an interesting writer, and one who raises numerous issues worth examination and discussion. In particular, his novel *Looking Backward from the Year 2000* (1973) and the "sequels" which followed it, provide a fascinating exercise in socioeconomic speculation: a genuine thought-experiment in Utopian engineering. It is worth noting that this is the only significant Utopian novel to be produced in the *genre* during the last forty years which does not tie its Utopian pretensions to some recommendation of "technological retreat."

Mack Reynolds was born in 1917, but did not embark upon his writing career until the late forties. His first sales to the SF magazines were made during 1949-50, and while the post-war magazine boom continued he sold stories regularly. He collaborated occasionally with Fredric Brown and once with Theodore Cogswell, and like these writers he concentrated mainly on light-hearted and humorous pieces. In 1951 he published an amusing and enjoyable novel called *The Case of the Little Green Men,* in which a failed private eye is hired by science fiction fans as part of an elaborate hoax, and becomes involved in a series of murders apparently committed by a superhuman agency.

Reynolds introduced himself to the readers *of Imagination* in 1952 in one of that magazine's "author profiles," and revealed that he had ambitions above and beyond what he had previously attempted to do in the *genre*: "What am I doing now? Writing a serious science fiction work which should take at least two years to complete. No wars of the future, no ray guns, extra-terrestrials, nor even time machines. It's going to be called *Tomorrow.*" If this project was ever completed it evidently failed to find a market, and eight years were to pass before Reynolds was again to attempt serious speculations about the near future. In 1960, though, his career entered a new and prolific phase as he began selling regularly to *Astounding*, which was at that time in the process of becoming *Analog* and cultivating a new image. In May of that year he published "Revolution," which carried a preface making a new declaration of intent:

> For some forty years critics of the U.S.S.R. have been desiring, predicting, not to mention praying for, its collapse. For twenty of these years the author of this story has vaguely wondered what would replace the collapsed Soviet system. A return to Czarism? Oh, come now! Capitalism as we know it today in the advanced Western countries? It would seem difficult after almost half a century of State ownership and control of the means of production, distribution, communications, education, science. Then what? The question became increasingly interesting following recent visits not only to Moscow and Leningrad but also to various other capital cities of the Soviet complex. A controversial subject? Indeed it is. You can't get much more controversial than this in the world today. But this is science fiction, and here we go.[1]

In the story an American agent is sent to Russia to give financial aid to a revolutionary underground, but becomes gradually anxious about what might happen *after* the revolution. When he learns that the revolutionaries plan to clear away the totalitarian state in order to set up a communist system owing much more fidelity to the ideas of Marx and Engels, he begins to wonder whether it might not be better to sell out his allies to the KGB.

A much more ambitious examination of the merits of the economic systems of America and Russia was "Adaptation," a short novel published in the August 1960 *Analog*. Here the crew of a starship is split by an ideological dispute regarding the best way to accelerate the historical and technological development of two "lost colonies" in the Rigel system. To put their claims to the test, the two factions take a world each and embark upon a project to civilize them in the shortest possible time. One group, favoring a Stalinist program of military conquest and accelerated industrialization planned by a centralized bureaucratic state, adopt the planet whose most advanced civilization is comparable to that of the Incas before the advent of Pizarro. The other, favoring a *laissez-faire* program in which technological innovations are to be distributed to merchants and entrepreneurs, adopts the planet whose most advanced culture is reminiscent of Renaissance Italy. (This arrangement seems hardly equitable but is, of course, convenient, in that post-Renaissance Europe was the birthplace of capitalism, and all revolutions so far accomplished in the name of communism have taken place—contrary to the Marxian theory of history—in more-or-less primitive countries whose economic systems have been of the types Marx categorized as Feudal and Asiatic.)

The story tells of the gradual involvement of the two teams in empire-building, and the transformation of the experiment into twin quests for personal power. As the bitter rivalry between the two factions threatens to break into all-out war between the two worlds, the situation is saved by the fact that the natives of both worlds, resenting their manipulation by the Earthmen, form an alliance to dispossess their masters of all their power. *Their* verdict on the great experiment is that whatever the best route of programs might be, and whatever the ideal economic system, there just *has* to be something better than the processes through which their worlds have been forced.

"Adaptation" is one of Reynolds's best works, and would have profited immensely from expansion into a more carefully analytical novel. It had, however, to find a home in a paperback market which was hardly renowned for its promotion of such projects, and in fact the longer version of the story—*The Rival Rigelians* (1967)—is simply inflated to novel length by the addition of some padding. It remains, of course, a straightforwardly iconoclastic work, attempting nothing more than a mocking indictment of two opposing ideologies which, in Reynolds's view, were pretty much as bad as one another. He ventures no suggestion as to what a better system might look like, but there is one significant point made in the climax. The crew of the starship, of course, come from an Earth much advanced beyond our own, and the political programs for technological and economic development they have been testing are taken from their rather distant past. One of the crew members volunteers to explain to the native leaders the *nature* of Earth's present economic system. They decline, apparently having little confidence in the likelihood of its being any better. This was Reynolds's conviction, too, about the imminent future of America and Russia—he thought that things might very well get worse instead of (or at least before) getting better. Much of his work during the sixties employs the premise that both Western capitalism and Eastern state socialism might follow a similar pattern of stultification.

In two other stories published in 1960, however, Reynolds deliberately espoused the "heretical" hypothesis that in the near future the Soviet system might work well enough to enable the East to outstrip the West. In "Combat" (*Analog*, October 1960), an alien starship lands in Russia because that nation has "the largest government and the most advanced on Earth," and the alien ambassador criticizes an American agent because his parent nation has adopted a strategy of attempting to retard Russian progress rather than trying to step up its own rate of progress to stay ahead. The premise is taken to absurd extremes in the comedy "Russkies Go Home!" (*The Magazine of Fantasy & Science Fiction*, November 1960; expanded as *Tomorrow Might Be Different*

[1975]), in which the Russian planned economy is booming to the extent that the Russians are dumping cheap goods throughout the West in order to obtain sufficient foreign currency to supply the needs of her tourists (who have replaced American tourists as the archetypes of arrogance and vulgarity). The hero plans to save the West by inventing a new ascetic religion which will put an end to tourism and conspicuous consumption if only it can be exported to the East. The Russians see through the plan quickly enough, but instead of opposing it they accept it greedily, because the first waves of Chinese tourists are already flocking to the fatherland of the revolution.

"Freedom" (*Analog*, February 1961) is much more serious in intent, suggesting that Russia's satellite countries might become gradually more liberal. A KGB agent sent to identify the origin of the subversive movements finds that they are not the product of anti-party conspirators, but the result of a spontaneous mass demand for freedom of speech. In the story, the agent himself becomes a subversive and learns to see the KGB as an oppressive and undesirable force. The fate of Dubcek's regime in Czechoslovakia seven years later testifies to the fact that the story was a little on the optimistic side.

In Reynolds's next *Analog* novella, "Ultima Thule" (March 1961; reprinted as part of *Planetary Agent X* [1965]), he again abandoned the near future of Earth in order to use one of the conventional backgrounds of postwar SF as a medium for a curious socioeconomic parable. The story hinges on the notion that the galaxy has been colonized after the fashion of Eric Frank Russell's *The Great Explosion*, with small social groups dissatisfied with conditions on Earth having blasted off to found their particular Utopias or to preserve their particular traditions. All conceivable political and economic systems are represented, their idiosyncrasies protected by the "United Planets Charter," which pledges that no one will attempt to interfere with anyone else's socioeconomic affairs. The United Planets organization, however, has a mysterious department called Section G, whose secret function is the subversion of the Charter. In the story, a new recruit to the department is assigned the task of tracking down "Tommy Paine," a mercurial mastermind who has been provoking revolutions throughout the galaxy. He finds out, eventually, that this is merely the *nom de guerre* used by the department to conceal its own activities.

The story has two interesting features. Firstly, its dialogue is mostly taken up by a series of challenges directed by a Section G operative at the hero's preconceptions related to the differential merit of various socioeconomic systems. His innocent liberalism is attacked and mocked as being essentially ethnocentric. Secondly, Section G is not fomenting revolutions in the name of any particular social policy—their revolutionary movements are as diverse as the regimes they overthrow—but simply in the name of *progress*. Implicit in the story is the view that any socioeconomic system is *"good"* if it is promoting technological progress, and bad if it is not. Tyranny is bad only because (or if) the oppressive apparatus of the state works to suppress creativity on the part of the intelligentsia. In "Ultima Thule" this view is rationalized by the fact that Section G has evidence that there is other intelligent life in the universe, technologically advanced far beyond the present ambitions of mankind, with which mankind might eventually have to compete. When the hero asks the head of Section G how he decides whether changes are for the better, he is told:

> It's sometimes difficult to decide, but we aim for changes that will mean an increased scientific progress, a more advanced industrial technology, more and better education, the opening of opportunity for every member of the culture to exert himself to the full of his abilities. The last is particularly important. Too many cultures, even those that think of themselves as particularly advanced, suppress the individual by one means or another.[2]

This is very much Reynolds's own credo. It forms the basis of his indictment of various images of near-future America, and it is the basic premise of his Utopian design in *Looking Backward from the Year 2000*. In "Ultima Thule" there is an immediate and practical motive for placing such a high priority on technological progress, but the aliens are really no more than a plausible excuse—a justificatory rationalization. In other stories this value-premise is simply axiomatic, or becomes entangled with Reynolds's notion of the "purpose of human existence." The premise is, of course, hardly new—it stretches back way beyond the technocratic propaganda of Gernsback to Francis Bacon's *New Atlantis*—but it cannot be said to have played an important part in the tradition of political philosophy since Plato and Aristotle. Where it *has* played an important part is in the covert sociopolitical assumptions built into modern science fiction, and in making it available for detailed examination Reyolds is to some extent providing a commentary on certain assumptions taken for granted by many of his contemporaries.

"Ultima Thule" ultimately became the source of a series of short stories and novels using the same background, and two other stories published in 1961 mark major points of departure in Reynolds's work. In "Farmer" (*Galaxy*, June 1961) he began to contemplate the future of the underdeveloped countries of North Africa and the role to be played by the superpowers in "aiding" their development. In "Status Quo" (*Analog*, August 1961; expanded as *Day After Tomorrow* [1976]), he made his first significant attempt to deal straightforwardly with the possible near future of the U.S.A. Neither story is impressive, the first being an account of the interaction of various political priorities involved in a project to reforest the Sahara and an attempt to sabotage the program, while the second presents an America obsessed by the twin notions of status and fashionability, where nonconformists (including the intelligentsia) are being slowly stifled. Both, however, set up the scenery for more interesting work.

"Farmer" was quickly followed by two short novels dealing with the future of North Africa, both of which ran as serials in *Analog*: *Black Man's Burden* (December 1961-January 1962) and *Border, Breed Nor Birth* (July-August 1962). It was not until ten years later that the two finally appeared in book form as halves of an Ace double, in 1972.

Black Man's Burden is built around a conference where the field-workers of various organizations and projects involved in providing "foreign aid" meet to discuss their prospects. Their declared purposes are various, but they share certain common aims which the more realistic among them are willing to state openly: the subversion of social institutions, the destruction of ways of life, the recruitment of labor for building, and the procurement of children for education. In order to help the tribesmen in all these ways the various groups are being forced to use subtle confidence tricks to cheat them out of their traditional patterns of culture. The purpose of the conference is to discuss the informal coordination of projects which, for political reasons, are insufficiently coordinated at the planning level.

Most of the agencies involved in these schemes use American negroes as their field-workers, because this is the only way that the various strategies they employ can be made to work, the tribesmen being extremely suspicious of white men. This, however, creates an awkward conflict of loyalties for many of the field-workers, who are totally dedicated to their work (and to the idea of progress) while finding much to despise in the cynical machinations of their white superiors, who are using African aid as an instrument of exploitation and as a diplomatic weapon in their "cold war."

The conference in *Black Man's Burden* reveals that an imaginary charismatic prophet, El Hassan, invented by one of the groups as an instrument of propaganda, has been taken up by some of the others, so that his name has been spread far and wide as that of a great reformer. After the conference, the group who invented him are recalled to base and given a new mission: to locate El Hassan and to figure out exactly where he stands. All the would-be manipulators want to find this new influential figure in order to co-opt him as a pawn. The heroes refuse to accept the new commission, deciding that it is time a new force entered the diplomatic field of play—one whose direct commitment is to the cause of African progress without being anyone's pawn. One of their number becomes El Hassan, and sets out to liberate North Africa. *Border, Breed Nor Birth* continues the story with an account of the first steps in this ambitious program, ending with the first great battle (against the Arab Legion).

The two stories are remarkable on several counts. Their subject matter was entirely new to the SF of the day (and there has been no significant attempt to develop it since). Some of its premises seemed particularly apt—the notion of the role played by American negroes in political dealings with Africa, for instance. (In the stories, the Communist bloc are handicapped because they have so very few black agents, but they do use Cuban troops—a minor point of prophetic success.) The plot of each novel revolves around the infiltration of El Hassan's cadre by agents commissioned to destroy it. In each case the agent is black, and in the second case much is accomplished by the defection of the agent to the cause. This pattern is repeated again in a third volume added to the series much later—*The Best Ye Breed* (1978)—and is also widely featured in Reynolds's other work dealing with subversive movements in Russia and America. *Black Man's Burden* and *Border, Breed Nor Birth* figure among Reynolds's most convincing work largely because it is easy to see exactly what the heroes are *fighting for*. Their political objectives are clear, because we know exactly what will *constitute progress* within the framework of the story, and what cultural forces act in opposition to it. The strength of Reynolds's commitment is easy to see, not only because of his recurrent use of the heroic turncoat as a key character, but also in his ready identification of the evils against which his characters must fight. These are the three major orthodoxies: the Eastern and Western versions of political orthodoxy and the Moslem version of religious orthodoxy.

The first two novels in this series suffered the disadvantage of not appearing in book form until they were out of date. *The Best Ye Breed* is less effective, for the same reason. There is a fourth story, "Black Sheep Astray," which Reynolds did for the John W. Campbell memorial anthology *Astounding* (1973), which deals with the ultimate fate of the successful El Hassan in the more distant future. It is neat enough in execution, but loses its pertinence and some of its strength because the political goals implicit in it are no longer so clear or so instantly acceptable.

As "Farmer" heralded the coming of a series of stories about the forces opposing progress in near-future Africa, so "Status Quo" heralded the coming of a series about the forces opposing progress in near-future America. This began with "Mercenary" (*Analog*, April 1962; expanded as *Mercenary from Tomorrow* [1968]). The situation envisaged here is much more bizarre than anything in Reynolds's straightforward stories about Russia or Africa, being more a caricature than a reasonable extrapolation. In order to indict trends in American society it was perhaps necessary for the author to make the image of American society held up for criticism clearly distinct from the America his readers knew and loved.

In "Mercenary" America's population is distributed into nine officially-recognized social castes, ranging from Upper-Upper to Lower-Lower through all the possible permutations of the designations Upper, Middle, and Lower. People inherit their status at birth, and with it their "occupational category." Most such categories have now become redundant because automation has taken over practically all manufacturing processes, and this means that for most people the possibility of status-promotion is negligible. The economic system of the future America is "People's Capitalism," and its major features are the protection of inherited wealth (which sanctifies and sustains the status-hierarchy), and the provision of social security for all citizens through the issue to everyone of shares in "Common Basic Stock." This Common Basic Stock originated when the government began taxing major corporations by appropriating some of their stock rather than cash from their profits. The dividends on these shares then became the source of all welfare payments, so that the fortunes of all citizens became linked to the fortunes of the country's major industries. This kind of system appears in virtually all of Reynolds's stories about near-future America, sometimes called "Guaranteed Annual Income" or "Negative Income Tax," and in his view constitutes a rationalization of the system which effectively exists at the present time. The logic of the situation is amply exposed in "Mercenary": because the great majority of people are unemployed, having been made redundant by technology, they are all dependent upon the income they get as a result of being small-time capitalists, and thus have everything to lose, in the short term, if anything should interfere with the smooth running of the system. The prospect of a revolution therefore seems remote—and yet the system holds back progress by sustaining a social hierarchy in which positions of importance are determined by the inheritance of wealth.

In the world of "Mercenary" there are two occupational categories in which it is potentially possible for Lower class individuals to win promotion: Category Religion and Category Military. The latter offers faster mobility at much higher risk, and also recruits constantly from other occupational categories. Wars are no longer fought in this particular future, the campaign for international disarmament having been so successful that all weapons invented later than the year 1900 are banned. However, the Category Military thrives because the entertainment-hungry American masses love watching small-scale battles on TV, and to supply this demand the curious practice has emerged of settling industrial disputes in trial by combat. (The disputes are, of course, between rival companies, not between companies and their workforces.) These "fracases" are bloody, and common soldiers suffer a high mortality rate, but promotion is relatively swift where genuine ability is there to be recognized.

The hero of "Mercenary" is Joe Mauser, determined to become the first man to win promotion into the Upper classes in many years.

As the story starts he is already a man of great competence, but his career has begun to stagnate because his ability and heroism have not caught the eye of the public. He is "adopted" by a TV cameraman who sets out to make him a star, and decides to take a big risk by signing on with the underdogs in a particular dispute, intending to win the battle against all the odds by a daring innovation whose legitimacy under the disarmament treaty is dubious. He wins the battle but loses his own private war, firstly because his employer dies and the son who inherits the company has transferred his own fortune into the shares of the rival company in anticipation of defeat, and secondly because his innovation is declared illegal. This second fact is not made known until the sequel to "Mercenary," *Frigid Fracas* (*Analog*, March-April 1963; published in book form the same year as *The Earth War*), which continues Mauser's story.

Robbed of his opportunity to reach the top, Mauser is transformed in the second story into a revolutionary. He is sent to the Soviet bloc—now dominated by Hungary—to contact the underground forces working against the Communist system with a view to coordinating operations. The intention is to prepare for the overthrow not only of the respective governmental systems, but also the rigid pattern of international relations which helps to sustain them: the "frigid fracas" (cold war). Mauser learns that Eastern Europe is in very much the same situation as the West, with the revolution having led to a status-hierarchy (the inner structure of the party) just as rigid and stultifying as that which has overtaken People's capitalism. Colonel Kossuth, the mouthpiece of the underground contacted by Mauser, offers the following synoptic "history" of the Soviet bloc:

> Stalin, in particular, but others too, both before and following him, were ruthless in their determination to achieve industrialization and raise the Sovworld to the level of the most advanced countries.... To accomplish these things, the Party had to, and did, become a strong, ruthless, even merciless organization, with all power safely—from its viewpoint, of course—in its hands. And, in spite of all handicaps and setbacks, eventually succeeded in the task it had set itself.... But then comes the rub. Have you ever heard, Major Mauser, of a ruling class, caste, clique, call it what you will, which stepped down from power freely and willingly, handing over the reins to some other element?.... A ruling caste, like a socio-economic system itself, when taken as a whole, instinctively perpetuates its life, as though a living organism. It cannot understand, will not admit, that it is ever time to die.[3]

In Reynolds's view, it is inevitable that the centralized State Bureaucracy of the communist countries will become a self-perpetuating, rigidly-stratified elite. The same, he suggests, may well be true of America. The conclusion of the Mauser/Kossuth debate and of the novel in which it appears is contained when Mauser reports back to his superiors as follows:

> I don't know why it didn't occur to any of us that the problems of the Westworld and those of the Sov-world at long last have become similar, almost identical. Both, following different paths, have achieved the affluent society, so called. But in doing it, both managed to inflict upon themselves a caste system that perpetuated itself eventually to the detriment of progress. In the past, revolutions used to be accomplished by the masses, pushed beyond the point of endurance. A starving lower class, trying to change the rules of society so as to realize a better life. But now, in neither West nor in the Sov-world are there any starving. The majority of Lowers and Proletarians are well-clothed, fed and housed, and bemused by fracases and trank pills, or their equivalent over there....
>
> The best elements in both countries have finally realized that changes must be made. These elements, the more capable, more competent, more intelligent, already are *running* each country though they are not necessarily Uppers or Party members."4

This message is repeated almost verbatim in the third novel in this series, *Sweet Dreams, Sweet Princes* (*Analog*, October-December 1964; in book form as *Time Gladiator* [1966]), which has a very similar theme focusing on a different hero. The scenario here is even more exaggerated, with the assumption that the masses are to be kept happy with bread and circuses given an exaggerated twist with the revival in America of gladiatorial games. All Reynolds's series deteriorate as they grow, and *Time Gladiator* is no exception, adding nothing new to the basic idea in terms of further extrapolation of the more interesting premise.

A very similar message to that contained in *Frigid Fracas* is featured in a novella which appeared at about the same time—"Speakeasy" (*F&SF* January 1963; expanded as *The Cosmic Eye* [1969]). This is, however, a hopelessly unconvincing story built around its punning title. In a conformist America of the future free speech is driven underground, into "dens of vice" set up so that amateur intellectuals can get high on political argument. The hero of the story is an out-and-out revolutionary who plans a lone career of terrorism, but finds out eventually that some of the political elite are already trying to figure out how to take the reins of power away from their oppressive governmental apparatus.

Reynolds's next novel after *Sweet Dreams, Sweet Princes* was the satire *Of Godlike Power* (*Worlds of Tomorrow*, June-September 1965; in book form 1966), in which he continued to pay attention to the matter of circuses to keep the masses entertained. The setting of this novel is the immediate future, and it features the confrontation between the status-conscious host of a radio program, Ed Wonder, and a lay preacher named Ezekiel Josh Tubber. Wonder manages to get Tubber on to his chat show, intending to hold him up to ridicule, and provokes him to extreme anger. The trouble is that Tubber's curses really work. He has already cursed "the vulgarity of women" and thereby destroyed the cosmetics industry and the fashion world, and now he curses radio and TV, destroying virtually all of the entertainment industry (the remainder of the popular media are taken care of in a series of afterthoughts).

In this novel it is not easy to see exactly where Reynolds stands. The "hero," Ed Wonder, is an unsympathetic embodiment of the value-system already satirized in "Status Quo," but Tubber's extremism takes him far beyond the bounds of reason. As in most satirical novels, it is easy to see what the author is attacking, but not so easy to see anything constructive beyond his iconoclasm. Tubber's cult runs a community called Elysium in the tradition of the Utopian experiments of Robert Owen and Josiah Warren, where the philosophy of consumerism has been cast out as wasteful and soul-destroying, but Reynolds—though he clearly admires the community—can hardly be said to be recommending its way of life. The main point which is made by the novel is a critical one, summed up by Tubber before he falls victim to the mob whose circuses he has taken away:

> Our best brains are utilized contriving...nonsense and then selling it. On top of that, we are using up our resources to the point that already we are a havenot nation. We must import our raw materials. Our mountains of iron, our seas of oil, our once seemingly endless natural resources have been flushed down the sewers of this throwaway economy. On top of it all, what do you suppose this sort of thing is doing, ultimately, to the intellects of our people? How can a people maintain their collective dignity, integrity and sense of fitness if they can be so easily coerced into desires for nonsense things, status symbols, nothing things, largely because the next door neighbor has one, or some third rate cinema performer does?[5]

To all of this Ed Wonder's objection is quite simple. This, he argues, is what people *want*. There is simply no demand for the simple life as lived in Elysium. Tubber replies:

> That's what people are *taught* to want. We must reverse ourselves. We have solved the problems of production of abundance, now man should settle down and take stock of himself, work out his path to his destiny, his Elysium. The overwhelming majority of our scientists are working either on methods of destruction, or the creation of new products which are people do not either need or want. Instead, they should be working upon the curing of man's ills, delving into the secrets of the All-Mother, plumbing the ocean's depths, reaching out to the stars.[6]

Wonder's view is, however, the more realistic. This is *not* what people want, whether or not they want or have been taught to want what they have instead. *Of Godlike Power* ends with all the curses withdrawn and Tubber running for political office. The end of the story is suitably ironic.

Up to this point in time (mid-1965) Reynolds had enjoyed no conspicuous success as an SF writer. He had sold a considerable amount of wordage to *Analog* but had published only one SF book (*The Earth War*). In 1965 there followed *Planetary Agent X*, containing "Ultima Thule" and another novelette which was intended for *Analog* but never actually appeared there. In the next three years, however, he published ten further paperbacks, and this change in his fortunes seems to have been associated with a change in policy. From *Space Pioneer* (*Analog*, September-November 1965; in book form 1966) his priorities seemed to become much more rigidly commercial. His novels had always been peppered with spies and duels, but these had usually been secondary to the main focus of interest within his stories. Now plot moved very much into the foreground of his stories, and socio-economic speculation was largely abandoned. He continued to use elements of his older scenarios—in particular, the United Planets background—but only for the sake of convenience.

Most of the fiction that Reynolds produced between late 1965 and the middle of 1969 is rather poor, the most striking example being the United Planets series, which got steadily sillier as it progressed through *Beehive* (*Analog* December 1965-January 1966; in book form as *Dawnman Planet* [1967]), *Amazon Planet* (*Analog*, December 1966-February 1967; in book form 1975), "Fiesta Brava" (*Analog*, September 1967; in book form combined with two short stories as *Section G: United Planets* [1976]), and *Code Duello* (in book form only, 1968).

In 1969, however, the flood dried up completely. Reynolds published no science fiction at all in 1971 or 1972, and only one short story in 1970. For ten years he had been the most prolific contributor to *Analog*, but after publication of *The Five-Way Secret Agent* (April-May 1969; reprinted in book form 1975), he disappeared from its pages for eight years, reappearing only in 1977 with *Of Future Fears* (October-December). Why this happened only Reynolds can say, but it is probably not unconnected with the fact that in 1970 his principal paperback publisher, Ace, was taken over, and for a while virtually suspended operations. When Ace's production got fully under way again in 1975 they released fourteen Reynolds in three years, and one is inclined to presume that this log jam had built up much earlier. This can hardly have been the only reason for Reynolds's sudden disenchantment with SF, but it may well have been a contributory factor. It is, however, undoubtedly significant that the first new work which Reynolds produced in 1973, when his science fiction began once again to appear in some quantity, was *Looking Backward from the Year 2000*. This suggests that there was, indeed, genuine disenchantment involved in his temporary resignation from the field, and that he returned with his more serious intentions renewed and revitalized.

Few of the stories which first appeared between mid-1965 and 1969 are worth more than a passing mention in the context of the present article. A series published under the pseudonym "Guy McCord" in *Analog* and reprinted under Reynolds's own name as *The Space Barbarians* in 1969 is an interesting "lost colony" thriller in which a barbaric culture modelled jointly on the tribes of the Scottish Highlands and the North American Indians fight against the attempts of otherworlders to exploit and civilize them. In the first part ("Coup," *Analog*, November 1967), the author's sympathies are well and truly aligned with the barbarians, but when he added the other two parts (both appearing for the first time in 1969), he was more concerned with helping his hero adjust to the inevitability and ultimate desirability of progress. Similar signs of a return to serious intent are found in the other two novels published in the magazines in 1969: *The Five-Way Secret Agent* and *The Towns Must Roll* (*If*, July-September; expanded as *Rolltown* [1976]). Both these novels helped to bridge the gap in Reynolds's career by introducing characters who reappeared in later novels.

The Five-Way Secret Agent features Rex Bader, an underdog in the affluent society of future America. The caricature status-hierarchy of "Mercenary" is no longer in evidence here, and much emphasis is given to the role played by computers in the running of the society (a theme introduced into Reynolds's work in the spectacularly bad *Computer War*, serialized in *Analog* in June-July 1967 and reprinted as a book the same year, and developed more thoughtfully in *The Computer Conspiracy*, serialized in *If* in November-December 1968). Bader, like most of the population, is living on Negative Income Tax while study-ing hard in the hope of getting a job in space, and meanwhile offering his services to any takers as a private detective. As there is no work whatsoever for private detectives to do, he is somewhat surprised to find himself hired by several different agencies simultaneously. He is commissioned by a client to contact various individuals in Eastern Eu-rope with a view to initiating a network of multinational corporations which will eventually take over the world. The mafia, the Inter-Ameri-can Bureau of Investigation, and a mysterious subversive organization called the Technocrats all hire him to betray this original trust, and he decides to complicate matters further by planning to play a hand in the affair himself. The story is implausible, but it is important within the developing context of Reynolds's work because it is, in a sense, a sce-nario-update of the future America envisaged in "Mercenary." Its mes-sage is in some ways similar to that of *Frigid Fracas*, but there is a new note of optimism in connection with the revised background. The spokesman for the emergent era who explains to Bader exactly which way the world is going repeats much of what Colonel Kossuth told Joe Mauser, but adds his own prospectus for a better future. The old po-litical elites are simply fading away because they are redundant, and the *real* power is now vested in the intelligentsia who are actually running things, and it is in the interests of East and West that they should com-bine forces:

> "Obviously, the cosmocorps are the future. Inter-national borderlines are no longer valid.... It will not be an overnight affair, but we must begin and the sooner the better. Urge Mr. Roger to push the inter-nationalization of communications bill through your Congress. If and when it passes, whether or not the Party would like it so, there will have to be an Inter-national congress to discuss the matter.... When and if the governments of both the West and the Soviet Complex have agreed, a new type of cosmocorps will have to be set up, possibly in Switzerland. Very well, Mr. Bader, that cosmocorps will be our point of con-tact with our fellows in the West. There we will lay our plans for future ventures."[7]

The "cosmocorps" referred to are, of course, the successors to the multinational corporations of today. It was in these institutions—and the fact that as productive endeavors they have to be run by intelli-gent people promoted on merit (Meritcrats)—that Reynolds saw in 1969 a possible way out of the impasse which he had discovered in "Mer-cenary" in 1962.

In *The Towns Must Roll* Reynolds addressed himself in a more optimistic frame of mind to the business of imagining a near-future America in which the millions made redundant by mechanization and living on Negative Income Tax can institute their own "mini-Utopias" by gathering together into communes and whole towns full of mobile homes which can migrate in search of new inspiration. The novel concerns the misadventures of one particular mobile town as it travels south through Mexico, awakening the envy and resentment of the local populace. Reynolds was later to expand the theme to cover a wider range of possible lifestyles in the novel *Commune 2000* (1974). Though not wholeheartedly Utopian, this notion of a "patchwork" society serving all possible idiosyncrasies was taken up by another writer determined to use SF as a medium for exploring Utopian possibilities, Ray Nelson, in the rather weak novel *Then Beggars Could Ride*.

Both *The Five-Way Secret Agent* and *The Towns Must Roll* may be regarded as in some sense setting the scene for *Looking Backward from the Year 2000*, in that they explore some of the ideas later to be used therein. The optimism which infuses them was clearly the motive force which led Reynolds to attempt the challenging project of designing a high-technology Utopia. Before going on to discuss the book, however, it is worth noting the one short story which Reynolds published in 1970, "Utopian," which was written for Harry Harrison's anthology *The Year 2000*, and which later became the starting point of one of the" sequels" to *Looking Backward*, *After Utopia* (1977). This sounds a cautionary note, in that it concerns a revolutionary of today brought forward in time into a Utopia of abundance by dissenters who feel that society is stagnating because life is too easy. This raises, in advance of *Looking Backward from the Year 2000* and its sequel *Equality in the Year 2000* (1977), the *next* question: after we achieve Utopia, what do we do then?

Looking Backward from the Year 2000 takes its title from Edward Bellamy's classic Utopian novel of 1888. It retains the same basic plot-structures and gives the same names to its central characters. The political philosophy which informs the two books is basically similar—identical assumptions are made concerning the principles of social justice embodied in the economic system, and concerning the distribution of wealth.

The main features of the society depicted in Bellamy's novel are as follows:

1. All incomes are equal, and this is not conditional on employment. People work because they want to, and are free to choose their jobs. Less pleasant occupations are made more attractive by shortening the number of hours to be worked, and manipulations of this sort are carried out according to the

       principles of regulation by supply and demand, so that no oc-
cupation becomes undersubscribed or oversubscribed. Where
there are still too many volunteers the most able candidates
are selected. Promotion within occupations is strictly meritocratic.

2.   The lack of economic incentives is compensated by competition
for honor and prestige. Effort is rewarded by praise and lack
of it discouraged by disapproval.

3.   The system of government is democratic, but the nature of its
political institutions is left rather vague. The government
has, however, "merged" its functions and its bureaucratic operations with those of the larger corporations, so that virtually all public services and manufacturing industries have effectively been nationalized.

4.   All problems of deviance have disappeared because all the economic motives for crime have been removed.

       All of these features are retained by Reynolds in his Utopian
design. The most obvious differences between his version of the year
2000 and Bellamy's are the very different level of technology and unemployment. (The two do, of course, go hand in hand.) Though Bellamy looked to the industrial revolution to provide the means of production necessary to facilitate the reorganization of society on socialist
lines, he had little to say about new sources of power or more sophisticated machines. His is essentially an economy of *moderation* rather
than an economy of abundance. Reynolds's is very much the latter—
power is available on an unlimited scale thanks to nuclear fusion, and
there is no resource crisis because unlimited power means unlimited opportunity to recycle everything that we use and to extract metals from
the earth and the sea. Thus, where Bellamy considered that there would
still be sufficient labor-intensive industry and bureaucracy to absorb a
large work-force, Reynolds foresees virtually all work being automated
and bureaucratic functions being handled by computers, thus leaving a
large majority of the citizens permanently and irredeemably unemployed. This creates a major problem of incentive—Bellamy's suppo-
sition that honor and prestige can supply an adequate substitute for economic incentive may be weak in any case, and it becomes dangerously
weak if there is nothing that most of the people can be honored *for*.
Thus, Reynolds is compelled to introduce a further factor into his vision of the future, which is the notion that all ambitious but currently
unemployed people spend most of their time in the pursuit of knowledge and educational qualifications in the hope of getting employment
or at least obtaining some prestige in their chosen academic field. Education is completely computerized, so that this kind of endeavor involves little more than constant confrontation with a computer terminal.

There is much in Reynolds's image of the year 2000 which reflects the interests and speculations of contemporary social philosophers, and in choosing the particular framework which he does, he emphasizes the extent to which modern "futurology" is, indeed, recapitulative of nineteenth-century Utopian speculation. Thus, *Looking Backward from the Year 2000* echoes Herman Kahn, Anthony Wiener, and Herbert Marcuse in its development of the idea of an economy of abundance; Daniel Bell, Alain Touraine, Jurgen Habermas, and John Kenneth Galbraith in its preoccupation with the production of knowledge and the function of knowledge as a crucial social resource. Though Reynolds, like Bellamy, leaves his notion of the merging of political and economic structures rather vague, one of his main sources of inspiration is clearly Galbraith's *The New Industrial State*. Both Reynolds's *Looking Backward* and its sequel are peppered with quotes from contemporary social philosophers and journalistic speculators.

There is, of course, much in Reynolds's novel which stands in stark contrast to various American sociopolitical ideologies, most particularly his insistence on the demolition of economic incentives. Economic exchange in this future America is arranged on what is virtually a barter system, the exchange rates pertinent to various products being assessed according to the labor theory of value. (The merits of the labor theory had been discussed previously by Reynolds in—of all places—*Amazon Planet*, where he was careful to point out that its originator was not Karl Marx but Benjamin Franklin.) If there is one idea in *Looking Backward to the Year 2000* which seems certain to offend most of the book's readers, it is the notion of equal incomes for *everyone*, regardless of position or productivity. When the hero of the book, who was a wealthy playboy before being put into suspended animation in the early seventies, hears that most the population is unemployed but nevertheless drawing the same salary as everyone else, he immediately suggests that they are parasites. His hosts, however, justify their society's adherence to the principle of "From each according to his ability, to each according to his need" as follows:

> "None of them are parasites, Jule. And neither are you. Today—forgive me for lecturing—today, in a computerized automated factory which produces, say, shoes, two or three men on a shift may supervise the production of a hundred thousand pairs of shoes a day. But it is not just the three men who are producing those shoes. It is the whole human race down through the centuries. If they were working alone, without the whole race backing them, it is doubtful if they could produce more than a pair or two of shoes apiece, per day. But they have inherited the efforts of a hundred thousand generations of their ancestors. A

million years ago an early man discovered how to use fire. Another devised the first crude stone tool. Many generations later, animals were domesticated, agriculture stumbled upon, the wheel invented, the use of metals begun. Man's background of knowledge increased and increased and soon every generation was contributing. This legacy of invention and development doesn't belong to one man nor to any group of men. It belongs to the whole race. As a result of it, we have finally reached the point where a fraction of our people can produce an abundance for all."[8]

This is the central tenet of Reynolds's political philosophy, here expressed for the first time in terms of a positive prospectus rather than a covertly-held position used as a standpoint for the criticism of dystopian regimes. Its basic claim is quite simple: progress, from the moment it first began, has been the work of the whole human race; it is essentially a collective endeavor. Its benefits, therefore, should accrue to us all, equally and without discrimination on the grounds of whether we are occupied in productive labor, or even the production of more progress. On this model, all of history consists of the efforts of individual men, social groups, and whole nations to seize for their own particular advantage what is really the common property of the race. This is not a view likely to have won the immediate approval of sympathizers with the American Libertarian movement—or, for that matter, from John W. Campbell, who once enthused about a series of openly didactic stories by Raymond F. Jones which suggested that Isaac Newton should have been able to patent the law of gravity, and that modern theoreticians who make equally important discoveries should keep their knowledge secret until they are allowed to patent them. (Isaac Newton himself, of course, was ready to admit that he had seen further than other men "by standing on the shoulders of giants," and had a craving for recognition which might have allowed him to fit in rather well in Reynolds's prestige-incentive society.)

There are, of course, several objections which can be raised with respect to the credibility of the societies designed by Bellamy and Reynolds, and perhaps the main weakness of Reynolds's book is the fact that in following its model so closely it fails to immunize itself against some fairly obvious criticisms. Bellamy's case rests upon numerous assumptions, of which three are especially weak. These are the assumptions that social approval and censure (whether formal or informal) can adequately substitute for economic incentives; the assumption that equal incomes for everyone will actually operate to cancel out envy and greed to the extent that there is no widespread social dissatisfaction or crime; and the assumption that the people who occupy positions of power will not use their power corruptly. These three assumptions are, of course, interlinked with one another, and eventually they can be traced back to the fundamental assumption that the evils that exist in our society are the result of flaws in social structure and organization rather than flaws in "human nature." Bellamy's view of man is thus markedly akin to that of William Godwin or Karl Marx, who saw human consciousness as a product of social conditions, and considered that in the appropriate social circumstances men would be happy, sociable, generous, and good. This contrasts starkly, of course, with other notions of human nature—for example, that assumed by another of the fathers of modern sociology, Émile Durkheim, who saw human nature as fundamentally a collection of insatiable desires which must be held firmly in check by powerful socially-imposed constraints. Whereas Marx saw contemporary social constraints as sources of "alienation" without which men could be free, Durkheim saw moral norms as essential to mental well-being, and argued that where they became weak men suffered from "*anomie.*"

Reynolds, in following Bellamy, clearly retains a basic commitment to the Marxian model of human nature, but it is interesting that throughout his work he seems to find some difficulty in believing it. It is his caution in accepting this particular item of faith which, more than anything else, is responsible for the range of his various alternative images of the year 2000, including *Commune 2000, Police Patrol 2000* (1977), and *The Towers of Utopia* (1975). Even in *Looking Backward from the Year 2000* and *Equality in the Year 2000* (which also takes its title from Bellamy), there is a curious prevarication with respect to this matter. The first book has an ironically unhappy ending when the hero realizes that there is no place in the new world for him because he cannot hope to get a job or to catch up the thirty-year gap in his education. In the sequel, this situation is resolved because Reynolds borrows from a novel which he wrote in the interim, *Ability Quotient* (1976), a technique for enhancing the power of the brain to enable it to absorb and take command of new knowledge at a vastly increased rate. However, in the second novel the hero meets up with a whole "underground movement" of dissatisfied individuals who wish to overthrow the meritocratic Utopia. The movement's plans are thwarted, but the very admission that such people *could* exist is a dangerous one which calls into question the assumptions upon which the society's Utopian claims rest.

In *Perchance to Dream* (1977) and *After Utopia* the doubts haunting Reynolds's *Looking Backward* crystallize out into a line of thought which leads inexorably to the collapse of the image. These novels were not the first in which Reynolds had extended his speculations about possible societies of the year 2000 to incorporate doubts about its Utopian potential, but they are the most damning. *Commune 2000* deals in a cursory manner with the possibility of political corruption on the part of the people who are in positions of real power (the people who run the computers), but is basically an optimistic work, while *The Towers of Utopia* examines some of the day-to-day problems which might arise in running the gigantic skyscraper-towns which play such an important part in the world of *Looking Backward*, never losing the conviction that such problems could be coped with adequately. *Perchance to Dream*, however, introduces a much more ominous note into the discussion.

The story features a new invention, the "intuitive computer," which is basically a machine for synthesizing experiences. These experiences can be reconstructions of actual historical events or pure fantasies, and the machine thus offers both the perfect means of historical "research" and the perfect vehicle for indulgence in "escapist" hallucinations. The hero of the novel spends alternative chapters using the machine to reconstruct the life of the Roman Horatius, whose fame was reinforced by the best-remembered of Macaulay's *Lays of Ancient Rome*, while the rest of the narrative is concerned with the rather inefficient attempts of various interested parties to steal it from him. The Roman sequences form a story that is one of Reynolds's best works, showing none of the faults of dialogue-construction and lifestyle-depiction which mar many of his near-future stories, and the novel obtained a couple of Nebula recommendations on the strength of it, but the book is really little more than a preface to *After Utopia*.

The hero of *After Utopia* is a dedicated member of a revolutionary organization whose nature is unspecified, but whose political ideology is generally anarchistic. He is in some mysterious manner "hypnotized" into stealing the movement's funds and putting himself into suspended animation so that he wakes up in the middle of the twenty-first century. His hosts are themselves aspiring revolutionaries who have brought him out of his own time in order to advise them as to how to overthrow their society, which is the world *of Looking Backward* half a century on and already decaying. The reason for the decay is that the lack of incentives provided for the vast majority of the people has resulted in the rapid spread of the intuitive computers, functioning as "dream machines." The entire population of the world seems to be on the brink of forsaking real existence altogether in favor of the infinite reaches of synthetic experience which the machines can provide.

The idea that a high-technology society might fall prey to this kind of fate is, of course, hardly new. In fact, it has been one of the perennial nightmares of twentieth-century science fiction. The notion of men whose needs are entirely supplied by machines becoming useless lotus-eaters forms the central argument of many indictments of pseudo-Utopian futures, from Forster's "The Machine Stops" through Miles Breuer's *Paradise and Iron* and Don A. Stuart (John W. Campbell)'s "Twilight" to Ira Levin's *This Perfect Day*. A premise virtually identical to that used by Reynolds in *After Utopia* was employed by Fletcher

Pratt and Laurence Manning in "The City of the Living Dead" in Gernsback's *Science Wonder Stories* in 1930.

The charges laid against such models of society as are presented by these stories assume that given the opportunity men will retreat from real life in pursuit of pure pleasure, stagnating psychologically, and taking society into the grip of total decadence. The reason, of course, that we find the prospect so horrible is that we find it so plausible: we can easily imagine ourselves falling prey to such temptation, and fear that we would find it irresistible even while our intellects rebelled against it. However, if the Marxian image of man were really viable, this fear would be chimerical, for it would only be alienated men who needed or wished for this ultimate opiate. In a "true" communist society these dream machines would be used purposively, as a source of intellectual stimulus and as an art form. *After Utopia*, unlike *Looking Backward from the Year 2000*, assumes the Durkheimian image of man whose insatiable desires will inevitably lead to self-destruction if not checked by external constraints.

The "solution" discovered by the hero of *After Utopia* is as commonplace (at least within the mythology of science fiction) as the problem. Section G of the United Planets organization rationalized their commitment to progress by reference to a prospective alien enemy, and *After Utopia* shares with another Reynolds novel published a few months later (*Space Visitor*, 1977) the assumption that if such an enemy does not exist it is necessary to invent one. The logic of the solution is simple enough: nothing assures social solidarity and commitment to purposive endeavor better than a state of war, or a state of high anxiety aroused by the prospect of war. There are, however, other sides to the question, one of which is featured in another recent Reynolds novel, *Galactic Medal of Honor* (1976; expanded from a 1960 novelette). This novel points out that preparedness for war may eventually create conflict where none need exist, and also that the commitment to production and self-sacrifice engendered by the threat situation will lead to the mass-production of things that ordinary men neither want nor need, thus wasting resources without any real gain in the quality of life.

What this confusion of viewpoints serves to emphasize is the circularity of the argument first set forth in "Ultima Thule," to the effect that progress is necessary in order that we might compete with possible enemies we might one day meet. In *After Utopia* and *Space Visitor* this becomes an obvious self-deception, for the alien enemy is here invented solely in order to establish a commitment to collective endeavor in the name of progress. In the final analysis, the commitment to progress is the one fundamental value-judgment that Reynolds makes, and all of his socioeconomic speculation seems once again to revolve around the argument which he put forward as the "moral" of "Ultima Thule"—that in the end just about any sociopolitical system can be justified if it encourages progress. Reynolds's one real doubt

71

about his Utopian vision as sketched out in *Looking Backward* and *Equality* is not that it might not arrive (he never claims more for it than that it is a possibility that *might* be realized if we work at it), but that it might lose its progressive impetus. When we realize this, we can see that *Looking Backward from the Year 2000* is, despite its politically controversial nature, a less subversive work than it might at first appear, for its frank espousal of the political ideology of egalitarian socialism is really a secondary issue. The book's first and foremost loyalty is to the mythology of progress, and it is this aspect of it which invites more detailed discussion in relation to sociological theories of social change.

One of the most striking weaknesses of both Bellamy's and Reynolds's Utopian novels is their vagueness in drawing a historical connection between future and present. In both cases the heroes ask in open amazement how on earth all this can have come about, and they are told with a shrug of the shoulders that it just happened, and that once it *had* happened it seemed so natural. Bellamy adds to this some oblique comments on processes of social evolution, but without specifying how these processes are governed.

Clearly, neither writer employs the Marxist theory of social change, which saw the process of history in the development of class-conflicts which could only be resolved by revolution and the metamorphosis of the economic system. On the other hand, neither writer assumes that some kind of teleological element is built into history. It is not obvious, moreover, how either writer interprets the word "progress." The advancement of knowledge and technology is a part of it, but not the whole, for both also consider that there is some kind of *liberation* involved—that men once oppressed by circumstances and by one another are being made free. Knowledge and technology, providing resources for the control of the environment, are a major part of this process of liberation, but not all—a necessary, but not a sufficient condition of it. What, then, is the remainder?

The idea of progress was a product of the Enlightenment, emerging first and most powerfully in pre-Revolutionary France. We find it occupying a central position in the social philosophy of all French writers of the period. Turgot, Condorcet, Saint-Simon, and Comte form a tradition of thought extending from the mid-eighteenth century to the mid-nineteenth, the central tenet of which was expressed by Condorcet in *The Progress of the Human Mind* (1794):

> Nature has set no term to the perfection of human faculties...the perfectibility of man is truly infinite; and...the progress of this perfectibility, from now on independent of any power that might wish to halt it,

has no other limit than the duration of the globe upon which nature has cast us.

It was this notion which informed the earliest of the futuristic Utopias (Mercier's *L'An 2440*, published in 1772, is the most famous). It was the same notion that impelled Hugo Gernsback to found *Amazing Stories* as a vehicle for Utopian "scientifiction" which would remind America of the perfectibility of man armed with the mechanical arts, and to feature such stories as Otfrid von Hanstein's *Electropolis* (1930) and Lilith Lorraine's "Into the 28th Century" (1930). By this time, however, the notion was already losing some of its glitter and its credibility, and the next twenty years were to see the decline and fall of the mythology of Utopian progress and the perfectibility of man. Bertrand Russell was among the first to put the case for the opposition when he wrote in 1924:

> Science has not given men more self-control, more kindliness, or more power of discounting their passions in deciding upon a course of action. It has given communities more power to indulge their collective passions, but, by making society more organic, it has diminished the part played by private passions. Men's collective passions are mainly evil; far the strongest of them are hatred and rivalry directed towards other groups. Therefore at present all that gives men power to indulge their collective passions is bad. That is why science threatens to cause the destruction of our civilization.

Here, what is taken for granted is the opposite of what was assumed by Condorcet and his allies: here it is the imperfectibility of man that is stoutly and confidently declared, and on that basis the value of technological advancement is challenged. It is here argued that the power provided by the growth of knowledge (which includes the power to manipulate the minds of men as well as the power to manipulate the environment) will necessarily be misused.

The predicament of Reynolds—the only contemporary science fiction writer to have made a serious attempt to design a Utopian society—becomes clear when we realize the extent to which his acceptance of the imperfectibility of man prejudices his Utopian optimism. We find it difficult to believe that the world of his *Looking Backward* could ever come about—and even he finds it difficult to believe that its pretensions could be sustained—because we can no longer accept what the Marquis de Condorcet took for granted.

What Reynolds must find, therefore, to add to the advancement of knowledge in order to make up his particular idea of progress, is some substitute for the myth of the perfectibility of man. This is what he does not seem to have, for when his characters are actually forced back to defining what they mean by progress, or what they consider to be the purpose of human endeavor, no such substitute features in their replies. Thus, for instance, the would-be American revolutionary in the short story "The Throwaway Age" (*Worlds of Tomorrow*, Winter 1967) can only reply, when asked about his ultimate aims:

> "I guess the ultimate goal, Paul, man's ultimate goal, is total understanding of the cosmos."9

It is not particularly surprising to find this statement of purpose being put forward by a science fiction writer, in that it can be said to be the implicit goal of all scientific endeavor, but it is not easy to see how it can be expected to stand alone as the focal point of *political* philosophy, without the addition of extra value-judgments about the constituency of the "good life" and hence about the way societies ought to be organized. There is some kind of additional commitment in Reynolds's philosophy of progress, because there has to be in order to render his speculations intelligible, but it remains both covert and uncertain. He cannot spell it out, perhaps because he is himself unsure of what it amounts to.

This examination of socioeconomic speculations in the work of Mack Reynolds has served to illuminate the problems which face all contemporary science fiction writers who deal in images of the near future. *Looking Backward from the Year 2000* may be the last desperate flourish of a kind of Utopian image that was once central to the mythology of *genre* SF, or it may be the first of a new wave of Utopian designs, but either way it serves to illustrate both the major cause for the decline of technological Utopianism and the major difficulty which has to be overcome by would-be designers of better societies in the context of today's intellectual climate. The abandoned myth of the perfectibility of man, and its replacement by the assumption of the essential corruptness of human nature, is fatal to the very idea of Utopia, and *any* vision of the future which purports to hold out hope for a better life has perforce to tie itself to some prescription for the redemption of human nature from that corruptness.

Many contemporary SF writers have made prolific use of the mythology of the superman, of various mythologies of rebirth and of ecological mysticism in this fashion, but close scrutiny of all of these strategies reveals nothing more than a clever jargon of apology: an ahistorical (and frequently transcendental) salvation mythology with no roots in actual possibility. Reynolds, for all his faults as a writer, is trying to confront historical problems without the aid of a pocketful of gaudy miracles of psychic readjustment. He is writing "social science fiction" rather than quasi-religious fantasy, and is still searching for actual historical possibilities rather than miracles to provide hope for the future. Perhaps one thing more needs to be added here, and that is the observation that because he is a science fiction writer he is a "Utopian" only in a special sense of the word. He is by no means a dogmatic Utopian trying to define *the* perfect society—he is an explorer among ideas, trying to find historical avenues which might lead us to better societies than the one we have now. He remains committed to the idea that societies change, and always will change, and that no stable state ever could or should last forever. His view of the future is that it holds many alternatives—a view which is implicit in science fiction when it is considered as a collective endeavor.

Curiously, for such a prolific author, Reynolds gives the impression of rarely being at ease in his work. He writes in a manner which makes for very easy reading (he once topped a popularity poll run by the *Galaxy* group of magazines despite the fact that those magazines were only his secondary market), but it often seems that his casualness masks a certain discontent. Certainly, there is an imbalance in his work between the interesting ideas and the crude plotting, and it is probable that this imbalance is the result of a compromise which he feels obliged to make in order to be sure that the work will be marketable. For reasons already pointed out, there is little scope in a mass-market *genre* like science fiction for the kind of socioeconomic speculations which are Reynolds's real interest, and in order to indulge himself in such imaginative adventures he has probably found it necessary simultaneously to pander to the demand for routine melodrama which controls the lower strata of the SF market. He is not the first writer to have made such a compromise, and he will certainly not be the last. If he reaches the stage where he finds it possible and profitable to sell the books that he is undoubtedly capable of writing, he may yet achieve a considerable reputation. In the meantime, his better books offer plenty of food for thought, and deserve more attention in academic circles than they have so far received.

VI.

OUTSIDE THE HUMAN AQUARIUM

THE FANTASTIC IMAGINATION OF CLARK ASHTON SMITH

Clark Ashton Smith was born in 1893 and died in 1961, having lived for almost all of his life on the outskirts of Auburn, California. He had three overlapping vocations, working as a poet, as a writer of fantastic short stories, and as a sculptor and graphic artist. These careers brought him relatively little financial reward; he probably made a significant income only from the second-named, and that only for a few brief years in the 1930s, when he wrote fairly prolifically for two pulp magazines, *Weird Tales* and *Wonder Stories*.

The stories which Smith produced during this brief professional phase constitute one of the most remarkable *oeuvres* in imaginative literature. They were reprinted in a series of collections issued by the specialist publisher Arkham House: *Out of Space and Time* (1942), *Lost Worlds* (1944), *Genius Loci* (1948), *The Abominations of Yondo* (1960), *Poems in Prose* (1964), *Tales of Science and Sorcery* (1964), and *Other Dimensions* (1970). The best of them were rearranged and reprinted in a series of paperbacks in the Ballantine "Adult Fantasy" series: *Zothique* (1970), *Hyperborea* (1971), *Xiccarph* (1972), and *Poseidonis* (1973), which helped to renew interest in Smith's work; various collations of his best works have been issued in more recent years. The last remaining vestiges of his fiction were eventually assembled in *Strange Shadows: The Uncollected Fiction and Essays of Clark Ashton Smith*, edited by Steve Behrends with Donald Sidney-Fryer and Rah Hoffman. Many of Smith's highly ornate and sometimes vividly erotic works suffered censorship at the hands of the magazine editors, but for some reason he did not correct the book versions; most of the originals were destroyed by a fire, but a few survived to be reconstructed for a series of booklets issued by the Necronomicon Press in 1987-88, whose six volumes are *The Dweller in the Gulf, Mother of Toads, The Vaults of Yoh-Vombis, The Monster of the Prophecy, The Witchcraft of Ulua,* and *Xeethra*.

From the viewpoint of modern critics and historians, Smith is one of three writers associated with *Weird Tales* in its heyday whose work stands out as being possessed of extraordinary originality. The other two—H. P. Lovecraft and Robert E. Howard—both died in the late thirties, but despite the fact that Smith survived them by a quarter of a century he wrote very little after that period. In a curious sense, Lovecraft's and Howard's deaths did not inhibit the extrapolation of their careers, because other hands took over where they left off, completing story-fragments they left behind and writing pastiches as close as possible in style and spirit to the originals. Lovecraft stands as father-figure to his own sub-*genre* of weird fiction, his "Cthulhu Mythos" having been used as a background by many other writers, while Howard is one of the key figures in the tradition of "sword-and-sorcery" fiction, and his violent heroes—most notably Conan the Barbarian—have continued their adventures in the care of other chroniclers. Smith has not been subject to necrophiliac attentions on anything like this scale, partly because he was always the least celebrated of the three writers and partly because his style is virtually inimitable. Although there are certain recurring patterns in his work, it has not the kind of homogeneity and stereotypy which would be capable of mass-production.

In terms of popular taste all three of these *Weird Tales* writers were ahead of their time. Their pioneering endeavors appealed in the first instance to a small corps of admirers, whose enthusiasm kept the work alive in the margins of the marketplace until the general evolution of fantastic fiction accustomed a much wider range of readers to the vocabulary of ideas with which they worked. The communicative efficacy of their work had to wait until an audience appeared whose context of understanding could be tuned in to their idiosyncrasies. There are still readers and critics who cannot abide one, two, or all three of them and who stigmatize key features of their work as evidences of bad writing. For this reason, Howard is often written off as a hack producer of fast-moving blood-and-thunder narratives; Lovecraft is taken to task for his stilted prose and piled-up adjectives; Smith is criticized for his love of exotic words and his highly-ornamented descriptions.

Such accusations tend to miss the point of the characteristics in question, each of which is a necessary corollary of the particular virtue and virtuosity of the writer's work. The pace and violence of Howard's work, and the adjectival awkwardness of Lovecraft's, are part and parcel of their distinctive moral and existential contexts. Critics out of sympathy with Howard's and Lovecraft's different varieties of quasi-paranoid worldview can hardly be expected to become connoisseurs of their literary development, but it is a pity that this has sometimes prevented the critics from recognizing that what they are seeing is unusual method rather than literary incompetence.

It is particularly necessary to make this point in discussing Smith's work, because although he too was extrapolating in his fiction a quasi-paranoid worldview, he was the most unusual of the three writers. Lovecraft was extrapolating a particular kind of anxious consciousness that was already detectable in the works of Edgar Allan Poe, Ambrose Bierce, and Robert W. Chambers, while Howard was offering a more hard-bitten version of a species of Romanticism already popularized by Edgar Rice Burroughs. Smith was not without literary forebears, and he was prepared to borrow from both Lovecraft and Howard, but his ambition was to go as far beyond his models as he possibly could. His phantasmagoric Decadent Romanticism was directed to the ultimate purpose of building dream-worlds stranger and more bizarre than had ever been described before. It was not enough for him to escape the mundane world; he wanted also to outdo in imaginative reach all the established mythologies of past and present.

Smith summed up this ambition in a prose-poem, "To the Daemon," where he offered up the following prayer to the fountainhead of his creativity:

> Tell me many tales, O benign maleficent daemon, but tell me none that I have ever heard or have even dreamt of otherwise than obscurely or infrequently. Nay, tell me not of anything that lies within the bourns of time or the limits of space; for I am a little weary of all recorded years and chartered lands....
>
> Tell me many tales, but let them be of things that are past the lore of legend and of which there are no myths in our world or any world adjoining.... Tell me tales of inconceivable fear and unimaginable love, in orbs whereto our sun is a nameless star, or unto which its rays have never reached.[1]

There is almost nothing in Smith's work of what is usually called "human interest." Those of his characters who live in the mundane world think of it as a drab and desolate place whose tedium is barely tolerable, and they are usually eager to take the opportunities which Smith's imagination offers them: to cross thresholds into worlds where the bizarre and the inexplicable are commonplace. Many of these fantasy-worlds are dangerous in the extreme, but the fascination which they exert on his protagonists is irresistible.

In the jargon popularized by J. R. R. Tolkien, Smith's stories are mostly set in Secondary Worlds which have their own "inner consistency of reality," but the most ambitious of them do not seem to have the customary relationship with the Primary World that most imaginary worlds in fantasy fiction have. These *milieux* exhibit neither the heroic permissiveness of Howardesque sword-and-sorcery fiction, nor the moral crystallization of Tolkienesque fantasy. The excuses offered in Tolkien's famous apologia for fantasy, "On Fairy Tales"—that Secondary Worlds provide for Recovery, Escape, and Consolation—are effectively scorned by Smith; there is no "eucatastrophe" in any of his most striking and heartfelt stories. His fiction is certainly escapist in its fashion, but the "freedom" which his protagonists win by their escape—and which is set to tantalize, by proxy, the reader—is freedom without security, strangeness without safety, and in many cases leads only to doom or bitter disappointment.

Smith did back up his work with a measure of aesthetic theory. He was prepared to defend, in articulate fashion, the notion that it was entirely proper for a writer to be unconcerned with the human world, or with such issues as careful characterization and the conventions of narrative realism. In a letter to *Amazing Stories* published in the issue for October 1932, he proposed that:

> Literature can be, and does, many things; and one of its most glorious prerogatives is the exercise of imagination on things that lie beyond human experience—the adventuring of fantasy into the awful, sublime and infinite cosmos outside the human aquarium.... For many people...imaginative stories offer a welcome and salutary release from the somewhat oppressive tyranny of the homocentric, and help to correct the deeply introverted, ingrowing values that are fostered by present-day "humanism" and realistic literature with its unhealthy materialism and earth-bound trend. Science fiction, at its best, is akin to sublime and exalted poetry, in its evocation of tremendous, non-anthropomorphic imageries.[2]

It is not obvious, however, that the kind of escape offered by Smith's fantasies is really all that "salutary and welcome," and its grimness is something which may invite further explanation. If a case is to be made for there being special merit in Smith's work, then his fiction may require an apology more far-reaching than those usually offered for fantastic fictions. Smith's fantasy lies, for the most part, beyond the range of Tolkien's apologia just as its exoticism extends beyond that of more conventional fiction. In order to pave the way for any such explanation and apology, it is necessary to look more closely at the nature, history, and sources of inspiration of Smith's work.

What we know of Smith's life, from memoirs penned by people who met him and from short biographies compiled by L. Sprague de Camp and Donald Sidney-Fryer, suggests that it was remarkable for its uneventfulness. Apart from his artwork Smith had no career, though financial necessity drove him to many short periods of casual labour. His parents were relatively elderly when he was born—his father was nearly forty and his mother some years older—and he lived with them until they died, his mother in 1935 and his father in 1937. He did not marry until he was in his sixties, though his biographers suggest that he had earlier love affairs, perhaps with married women. Once the family moved into the small house which his father built on lonely Boulder Ridge in 1907, Smith very rarely left it until he married—visits to friends who lived further away than Auburn seem to have been very few and far between. Although he was highly intelligent, and read voraciously, Smith never attended high school or college, preferring to educate himself.

Despite this virtual isolation, however, there was nothing parochial about Smith's view of the world. In his correspondence he gave every indication that he loathed Auburn, and longed to be elsewhere, and yet he never left it. When he was in his twenties his health broke down, and for eight years between 1913 and 1921 he was unwell, suffering from various aches and pains and from periodic bouts of fever. A local doctor tentatively diagnosed tuberculosis, but de Camp considers this diagnosis to have been unreliable. By the time he had regained his health (and he recovered it sufficiently to undertake some hard manual labors in subsequent years), Smith may have felt that he was bound to Boulder Ridge by the aging of his parents, who needed to be looked after, but it is not easy to say why he did not leave Auburn once they were dead—or, for that matter, why he accomplished almost nothing during the remaining quarter-century of his life. Almost all of his best poetry, and all of his best fiction, was written before 1935.

Smith's interest in the exotic began, it appears, at an early age. He was a precocious child, and records in his brief autobiographical statements (written for the pulp magazines in the thirties) that he began to write in his early teens, producing many oriental fantasies. His interest in the Orient had apparently been provoked by reading the *Thousand-and-One Nights* at the age of eleven. At the age of thirteen his interest in the exotic was further encouraged by his discovery of Edgar Allan Poe, whose poetry was an important early influence on his own. At fifteen he discovered the work of the California poet George Sterling, who was to become an important influence and eventually a friend.

Though George Sterling is almost forgotten today, he published frequently in the popular middlebrow magazines of his day and was a celebrity on the west coast; his major collections were each reprinted several times during the 1900s. Smith sent some of his poems to Sterling in 1911, at the suggestion of a schoolteacher friend, and began a correspondence which led to a meeting in 1912. At that time Smith stayed with Sterling in Carmel for about a month, and met other admirers who had formed a kind of coterie around him. Shortly afterwards Smith came briefly under the wing of would-be patron of the arts Boutwell Dunlap, who took him to San Francisco and introduced him to the publisher A. M. Robinson, who issued Smith's first book, *The Star-Treader and Other Poems* (1912). This brief venture into the wider world was never repeated, perhaps because of Smith's health troubles. He continued, though, to correspond with Sterling and several other writers, building up a network of pen-friends which was eventually to include H. P. Lovecraft and Robert E. Howard.

George Sterling wrote prefaces for Smith's self-financed second and third volumes of poetry, *Odes and Sonnets* (1918) and *Ebony and Crystal* (1922), but he ceased to exercise any direct influence on Smith when he died in 1926, having taken poison—though Smith apparently doubted that he had really committed suicide.

There is a sense in which some of Smith's work takes over where Sterling left off, and Smith was influenced in particular by two of Sterling's poems: "A Wine of Wizardry" and "The Testimony of the Suns." The former poem, which first drew Smith's attention to Sterling when it was published in *Cosmopolitan* in 1907, describes in a fashion made literal by its mode of presentation a flight of Fancy, which takes her at hectic pace through various mythological scenarios of dark and Satanic character until she quits the earth entirely and sets forth for a distant star. At the end of this peculiar odyssey the poet, despite the fact that his vision has shown him that the world of the imagination is redolent with sinister and malignant figures, declares himself well content to have indulged in its intoxication. "The Testimony of the Suns" had been the title poem of a collection first issued in 1903; it ventures even further into distant realms of the imagination, and Smith wrote that it contained

> ...lines that evoke the silence of infinitude, verses in
> which one hears the crash of gliding planets, verses
> that are clarion-calls in the immemorial war of suns
> and systems, and others that are like the cadences of
> some sidereal requiem, chanted by seraphim over a
> world that is "stone and night."[3]

Though these two poems are exceptional in Sterling's canon, they are not entirely without echoes in the work of other California poets. The work of another sometime resident of Carmel, Edwin Markham (a much older man than Sterling, having been born in 1852), includes much religious poetry of a visionary nature, and Markham was ultimately to produce a spectacular supernatural odyssey of his own in "The Ballad of the Gallows Bird," published in the *American Mercury* in 1926. This long poem includes a transit of Hell and is replete with morbid imagery, as when skeletons erupt from their graves. These poems remind us that Smith's work—though undeniably extraordinary—is by no means entirely disconnected from the culture of its place and time.

Sterling knew Markham well (Markham wrote the poem "Sarpedon" in Sterling's memory), and he was also well acquainted with

Ambrose Bierce, the most famous of all the Californian writers of the day, to whom he showed some of Smith's poetry. Both Markham and Bierce must be counted among Sterling's influences, and hence among Smith's. Of greater importance, however, in determining the shape of Smith's career as a poet were more distant influences upon "A Wine Of Wizardry" which Sterling called to Smith's attention: influences from French literature.

Sterling apparently introduced Smith to Baudelaire's *Fleurs du Mal*—in English translation—in 1912, and impressed him sufficiently to inspire him eventually to learn French in order to be able to translate such works for himself. The Arkham House volume of Smith's *Selected Poems* includes along with thirty translations and "paraphrases" of Baudelaire translations from several other writers, including Paul Verlaine, Victor Hugo, José María de Heredia, and Charles Leconte de Lisle (as well as some fake "translations" which are actually Smith's own pseudonymous work). He seems to have discovered a strong affinity with the particular current in nineteenth-century French poetry which extended from the lusher products of Romanticism to the morbid extravagances of the Decadent Movement.

Many nineteenth-century French writers had a profound fascination for the Orient, which drove many of them actually to undertake eastward voyages (though few got any further than North Africa). There was also a prolific and potent supernatural element in nineteenth-century French literature, where the influence of Poe was supplemented by the influence of such English writers as Edward Young (whose *Night Thoughts*, translated by Letourneur in 1769, had been very popular) and Lord Byron. A "*genre macabre*" was extrapolated from collections by Théophile Gautier—notably *La Comédie de la Mort* (1838)—into the work of Baudelaire, Petrus Borel, and Gérard de Nerval's "*supernaturaliste*" poems. The slightly less fevered "Parnassian" poets also made abundant use of mythological material, to which Leconte de Lisle added a broad cosmic perspective strongly influenced by the evolutionist ideas of the day. Many writers of the period, influenced by the fashionable idea that genius was closely akin to madness, were happy to borrow inspiration from delirium, whether it was visited upon them by accidents of fate (like Alfred de Musset and Gérard de Nerval), or whether they had to induce it by other means with opium, hashish, or even ether (as Baudelaire, Gautier, Rimbaud, and Jean Lorrain were interested to do).

All of these concerns are echoed in Smith's work. He presumably came by his interest in Oriental and supernatural exoticism independently, and it is probable that his acquaintance with drugs was limited to those opiates which were used as pain-killers and sleeping-draughts, but he must have found a wonderful coincidence of outlook in the work of the French poets. He probably did not have the opportunity to familiarize himself thoroughly with the abundant short fiction produced by writers associated with the Decadent Movement—most notably Remy de Gourmont, Jean Lorrain, Marcel Schwob, and Catulle Mendès—but he would have found common cause with them too, and there is a sense in which Smith may be regarded as the last and most extravagant of the masters of Decadent prose.

Another element of the French literary tradition which may warrant consideration in the light of its influence on Smith's work is its religious context. France was a country very much aware of its Catholic traditions (always under stress after the revolution of 1789), and the atheists among the above-named writers formed their atheism in opposition to Catholic theology. Although reconsideration led some Decadents back from their literary flirtations with evil to a kind of repentance—Verlaine and Joris-Karl Huysmans are the cardinal examples—others remained firmly committed to the flagrant literary Satanism of Baudelaire and Anatole France. The Catholicism whose mythology provided the metaphysical context of all this work—even, and perhaps particularly, that which was moved by a spirit of strident opposition—was a Catholicism heavily influenced (thanks to Pascal, Racine, and Alfred de Vigny) by the desolate worldview of Jansenism.

Jansenists believed that man had been abandoned by an indifferent God, so that all that a cosmic voyage of the imagination could possibly reveal was a bleak and impassive universe, empty of any real comfort. Smith had no apparent links with the Catholic faith (although Sterling had; his parents had tried unsuccessfully to bring him up in the faith), but he nevertheless acquired and carefully extrapolated a worldview which was in close correpondence with the Romanticized Jansenist pessimism of the French tradition.

In his own poems, Smith sent his Fancy on more extended flights than Sterling's ever took, into the remoter regions of the imagined universe, where it found a multitude of monstrous and baleful apparitions, and an inimitable cold indifference which could offer no comfort to mankind. In "Nero," which led off his first collection, Smith imagines the Roman emperor wishing that he were a god, so that he could supervise the conflict of Chaos and Creation, and play with the stars so as to "tear out the eyes of light." Though such a god is not the quiet, hidden God of the Jansenists, he is certainly a deity which offers cold comfort to mankind. In the title-poem of that first collection, "The Star-Treader," the dreaming narrator is given a similar god's-eye view of the universe, and finds a similarly bleak awe in its rapt contemplation. Cosmic perspectives which reduce the earth and its inhabitants to insignificance are offered also in the "Ode on Imagination" and "The Song of a Comet."

In *Ebony and Crystal* this interest in cosmic perspectives—and particularly in the lushness and bizarrerie of the visions available to such perspectives—reaches fuller flower. Its most extended development is to be found in Smith's longest, and perhaps finest, poem: "The

Hashish-Eater; or, The Apocalypse of Evil," which begins with the memorable lines:

> Bow down: I am the emperor of dreams;
> I crown me with the million-colored sun
> Of secret worlds incredible, and take
> Their trailing skies for vestment when I soar,
> Throned on the mountain zenith, and illume
> The spaceward-flown horizon infinite.[4]

The intoxicating wine of wizardry which dispatched George Sterling's Fancy clearly had less impetus than the hashish which impelled Smith's emperor of dreams. Sterling's vision is essentially a syncretic amalgam of Earthly myths; to this Smith adds a breadth borrowed from the discoveries of astronomy and speculations of cosmogony, but he adds too a particular viewpoint in which the extremism of the vision is both necessary *and inadequate* to answer the pangs of imaginative suffocation and stultification. The violent and macabre elements of Smith's vision—its decadent dalliance with satanic imagery—are provocations to an imagination which (it is implied) could not be drawn to awe by any lesser stimulus. For Smith, conventional appeals to the imagination are effete and jejune. This is where Smith found his intellectual kinship with Baudelaire and Rimbaud: for them too the ultimate enemy of the human soul was not evil but *ennui,* and they too sought release from spiritual anaesthesia in magniloquence of vision and cultivation of mordant exoticism.

The influence of Baudelaire is most clearly seen in the twenty-nine poems in prose which Smith published in *Ebony and Crystal.* Indeed, the first of these to be published (in *The Smart Set* in 1918) is entitled "Ennui"; like "Nero" it features an emperor for whom earthly pleasures are inadequate to secure any spiritual release. Here, though, the emperor is brought to momentary sensation not by dreams of godhood but by a close brush with death.

These poems in prose contain the seeds of much of Smith's later fantastic fiction. It is not just that some of his stories are built around images recapitulated from the prose-poems ("The Demon of the Flower" around "The Flower-Devil," and "The Planet of the Dead" around "From the Crypts of Memory"), but that it was in the prose-poems that he cultivated the tone and worldview of so much of his later prose fiction.

The way in which Smith developed his poetry in prose has both significant similarities and important contrasts to the way that French prose-poetry developed from Aloysius Bertrand's *Gaspard de la Nuit* through Baudelaire's *Petit Poèmes en Prose* to Rimbaud's *Illuminations.* Bertrand's Medievalism gave way to the more varied exoticism of Baudelaire, and Baudelaire also began to produce more extended prose-poems, notably "L'Invitation au Voyage," whose theme is recapitulated by Smith in "In Cocaigne." Rimbaud was not much concerned with the further development of Baudelaire's exoticism, but he did import a special kind of fervor into the form, seen especially in some of the most memorable passages of the patchwork prose-poem *Une Saison en Enfer*—a kind of horrified rage which ultimately comes to delight in delirium and celebrate "the alchemy of the word."

The manner in which Smith's work sets off in a different direction is to do with his adoption of a rather different *mythos*, which draws upon the fantasies of science. It was not simply the *largeness* of the cosmic perspective which impressed him, but also the detachment and clinicality of the scientific outlook, and its calmness in confrontation with the alien and unimaginable. In this respect he is a distinctly twentieth-century writer, and though the work he did for the science fiction pulps is mostly weak by comparison with his *Weird Tales* stories, he nevertheless drew something important from the scientific worldview. For most pulp SF writers (and, for that matter, most scientists), the modern worldview simply invalidated all the fabulous beings of ancient mythology, and so SF writers developed their own distinct vocabulary of ideas; for Smith, though, it was only the attitude of mind which one adopted to demons, sorcerors, satyrs, and the like which needed to be transformed: he could achieve a remarkable synthesis of scepticism and credulity, which is one of the unique features of his work.

In discovering this new direction, Smith was of course aided by one of his American literary heroes, Edgar Allan Poe, whose own poems in prose presumably influenced Baudelaire. Like Smith, Poe had also imbibed something of the scientific worldview, and was himself given to cosmic visions, but in Poe there is no synthesis—such works as "A Mesmeric Revelation" and *Eureka* remain quite distinct from his tales of the supernatural. Only in the extended prose-poem "The Masque of the Red Death" do we find in Poe's work a real precursor of Smith's fiction.

What Smith shares most intimately with the French tradition is his notion of the goad which drives the imagination to construct rhapsodies in prose, one of whose facets is *ennui*, another *spleen*. One may borrow (taking it, admittedly, out of context) Rimbaud's reference to the "alchemy of the word" to describe Smith's method, because he was a great exponent of the alchemy of words. He used his vocabulary to transform descriptions into incantations directly, evoking a sense of the strange, a distortion of attitude and feeling. Smith's prose is geared to apply to the reader an experiential wrench or jolt, to permit the relief of "seeing" worlds of the imagination—which might otherwise have gone stale along with the hopeless world of mundanity—through a new linguistic lens. This is what his best prose fiction intends to accomplish.

Smith's earliest ventures in the marketing of prose fiction were tales of the Orient written in his late teens. Four were published in *The Black Cat* and *The Overland Monthly* during 1910-12. Some ten years later Smith began writing light contemporary fiction aimed at "sophisticated" magazines, but the only one known to have sold was "Something New" in *10 Story Book* in 1924. His earliest experiments with extended poems in prose, the brief but highly ornate fantasies "Sadastor" and "The Abominations of Yondo," were produced soon afterwards, in 1925. Both were submitted to *Weird Tales* but rejected by editor Farnsworth Wright. "The Abominations of Yondo" appeared in *The Overland Monthly* in 1926. Smith did try his hand at material in a more orthodox *Weird Tales* vein, selling "The Ninth Skeleton" to Wright in 1928, but it was not until 1929 that he established a better working relationship with the editor, which encouraged him to produce more adventurous material. In 1930 Smith had five stories in *Weird Tales* (including "Sadastor"), and also placed two stories with Hugo Gernsback's SF pulps. Thus began Smith's prolific phase, which lasted from the autumn of 1929 until the spring of 1934 (although the stories continued to appear in print for some years thereafter).

"Sadastor" and "The Abominations of Yondo" both prefigure clearly the direction in which Smith's work would develop. The first begins as an Oriental tale, with a demon telling a story to amuse a fretful lamia, but the story concerns a "forgotten and dying planet" set "among the remoter galaxies." The same ambition is confirmed in the opening lines of "The Abominations of Yondo":

> The sand of the desert of Yondo is not as the sand of other deserts; for Yondo lies nearest of all to the world's rim; and strange winds, blowing from a gulf no astronomer may hope to fathom, have sown its ruinous fields with the gray dust of corroding planets, the black ashes of extinguished suns. The dark orb-like mountains which rise from its wrinkled and pitted plain are not all its own, for some are fallen asteroids half-buried in that abysmal sand. Things have crept in from nether space, whose incursion is forbid by the gods of all proper and well-ordered lands; but there are no such gods in Yondo, where live the hoary genii of stars abolished, and decrepit demons left homeless by the destruction of antiquated hells.[5]

This passage might serve as an introduction to Smith's work in general, promising as it does a blending of the notions of the satanic and the alien.

The location of Yondo in space and time is vague, and in his early days Smith had some difficulty finding an appropriate *milieu* for his fiction. "The End of the Story" (1930) was the first of numerous stories which Smith set in the imaginary French province of Averoigne. It is a standardized story of a young man's seduction by a lamia, and of his determination to return to her embraces even after he has been "saved" from her attentions by an older and wiser man. It echoes the theme of Keats's "Lamia" and several stories by Théophile Gautier (especially "Clarimonde" and "Arria Marcella"), and has a similar outlook to Gautier's tales, which celebrate the superiority of deliciously dangerous supernatural consorts over mere mundane women.

In his subsequent tales of Averoigne Smith was able to recapitulate his enthusiasm for French Romanticism, sometimes coming close to pastiche. He is frequently close to the spirit of Anatole France's tales in *The Well of St. Clare*—especially "San Satiro"—and "The Disinterment of Venus" seems to have been inspired by Prosper Mérimée's "The Venus of Ille." An imaginary French province was, however, too close to home to accomodate Smith's wilder imaginings, even when he imported an alien invader (in "The Beast of Averoigne," 1933). Only in "The Colossus of Ylourgne" (1934) was his taste for the bizarre allowed full rein, though "The Holiness of Azédarac" (1933) shows off his sense of irony to good advantage in a tale which borrows from Robert W. Chambers's "The Demoiselle d'Ys" and from H. P. Lovecraft.

The other scenario used in an early tale which was to be further explored was Atlantis, featured in "The Last Incantation" (1930). This is another extended poem in prose, in which the sorceror Malygris, suffering from *ennui*, conjures up an image of a lost love, but cannot recover the innocence of viewpoint which made the girl so beautiful in the sight of his earlier self. "The Uncharted Isle" (1930) is a timeslip story which also seems to feature a fragment of an Atlantean civilization, though this is not stated. "A Voyage to Sfanomoë" (1931) is an interplanetary story which begins in Atlantis, but the exoticism of Atlantean sorcery is only displayed to its fullest advantage in "The Double Shadow" (1933) and "The Death of Malygris" (1934), which are both stories in which curious supernatural dooms claim the main characters—a favorite Smith formula.

In order to find more open imaginative territory Smith borrowed another mythical civilization from Greek mythology: Hyperborea, which he first featured in "The Tale of Satampra Zeiros" in 1931. This is the story of two thieves who attempt to plunder a shrine erected to the dark god Tsathoggua in a city which now lies in ruins; they are unwisely undaunted by the evil reputation which the place has. The protagonist escapes, though not intact, after seeing his companion horribly killed.

The characterization of the evil god in this story owes something to H. P. Lovecraft, to whose Cthulhu Mythos Tsathoggua is sometimes attached. The formula of following the fortunes of characters who invite awful supernatural judgment with their recklessness is here rendered in a sarcastic vein, and this appears to reflect the fact that—as in many of the Averoigne stories—wherever Smith consciously borrowed from other writers his tone tended to become more ironic, and sometimes rather flippant, his auctorial voice being distanced from the substance of the tale.

The irony of the Hyperborean tales (in the first of his Arkham House collections, *Out of Space and Time*, they are aptly dubbed "Hyperborean Grotesques") was something which Smith chose to conserve and exaggerate when he used the setting further. "The Door to Saturn" (1932) describes how the priest Morghi pursues the sorceror Eibon through a doorway to another world, where they combine forces in order to explore until they find a place to settle down. This is one of the least violent and most sardonic of all Smith's stories. It also includes some of his most tongue-wrenching nomenclature—a trend continued in "The Weird of Avoosl Wuthoqquan" (1932), which follows the familiar pattern of reckless greed leading to macabre extinction, as do "The Ice-Demon" (1933) and the magnificently bizarre "The Coming of the White Worm" (1941).

Less irony is to be found in "Ubbo-Sathla" (1933), the most Lovecraftian of the Hyperborean stories, in which a modern occultist finds a magic lens which unites him with the personality of its wizard owner, and allows him to share that owner's visionary quest to find the parent of all Earthly life, in which is incarnate Smith's typical blend of the evil and the alien:

> There, in the gray beginning of Earth, the formless mass that was Ubbo-Sathla reposed amid the slime and the vapors. Headless, without organs or members, it sloughed from its oozy sides, in a slow, ceaseless wave, the amebic forms that were the archetypes of earthly life. Horrible it was, if there had been aught to apprehend the horror; and loathsome, if there had been any to feel loathing. About it, prone or tilted in the mire, there lay the mighty tablets of star-quarried stone that were writ with the inconceivable wisdom of the premundane gods.[6]

By contrast, the most savagely ironic of the Hyperborean tales is "The Testament of Athammaus" (1932), told by a hapless headsman who is called upon to execute a demonic bandit. Each time the task is complete the bandit miraculously rises from the dead, and each time his head is struck from his shoulders he becomes more loathsome, until his hideousness forbids further interference. Like "Ubbo-Sathla" this is essentially a tale of devolution—a regression from order toward chaos (a devolution which is, in a sense, implicit in the very nature of the stories as they use a modern viewpoint to look back at a more disturbed and rough-hewn era).

All these chief elements of the Hyperborean tales are combined in the best of them all: "The Seven Geases" (1934). Here the vainglorious magistrate Ralibar Vooz goes hunting for extraordinary prey, but falls prey himself to the wrath of the sorceror Ezdagor after venturing into a strange underworld. Ezdagor places him under a geas which requires him to descend further into the Tartarean realm to present himself as a blood-offering to Tsathoggua. But Tsathoggua has no need of him, and so sends him further on, and the pattern repeats. In the company of the bird-demon Raphtontis, Ralibar Vooz delivers himself in turn to the web of the spider-god Atlach-Natha, to the palace of the "antehuman sorceror" Haon-Dor, to the Cavern of the Archetypes, and to the slimy gulf of Abhoth, "father and mother of al cosmic uncleanliness":

> Here, it seemed, was the ultimate source of all miscreation and abomination. For the gray mass quobbed and quivered, and swelled perpetually; and from it, in manifold fission, were spawned the anatomies that crept away on every side through the grotto. There were things like bodiless legs or arms that flailed in the slime, or heads that rolled, or floundering bellies with fishes' fins; and all manner of things malformed and monstrous, that grew in size as they departed from the neighbourhood of Abhoth. And those that swam not swiftly ashore when they fell into the pool from Abhoth, were devoured by mouths that gaped in the parent bulk.[7]

By this time, though, the magistrate is in a realm so remote that his own ordered world is known only by vile rumor, so Abhoth can think of no more awful place to send him than home. Alas, the journey back is fraught with far too many dangers for it to be safely made, so Ralibar Vooz, who is too puerile even to be worth devouring, cannot capitalize on the good fortune of his insignificance.

Here, despite the ironic voice with which the story opens, Smith is clearly carried away by the impetus of his constructed nightmare, and this is a key story in his *oeuvre*. The descent into the underworld is a fine representation of the metempirical reality in which Smith embeds his fantastic tales. The revelation that the ultimate reality is utterly loathsome is, of course, something which Smith echoes from Lovecraft's tales, but Smith's version is far more elaborate and far more colorful. Lovecraft is essentially a monochrome writer, but Smith's imagination is lush and fecund—his universe is not simply a horrific one, but a multitudinously *populous* one, in which there are not merely more things than are dreamt of in the Lovecraftian philosophy, but more things than are dreamt of in *any* philosophy.

This can be seen well enough in Smith's work for the SF pulps. It is surprising, in a way, that Gernsback made room in his magazines for a writer so ill-fitted to his declared manifesto (to the effect that SF was a futurological species of fiction which would anticipate technological developments), but Smith did have an imaginative verve which enlivened the pages of *Wonder Stories* quite considerably. His first story there, "Marooned in Andromeda" (1930), set the pattern for many others, featuring an odyssey across an alien landscape replete with strange life-forms.

Some of these stories of strange alien life-forms are hard to distinguish from his horror stories of vile godlings and devolved protoplasmic entities—"The Immeasurable Horror" (1931) and "The Vaults of Yoh-Vombis" (1932) both appeared in *Weird Tales* despite being notionally science fiction, and "The Dweller in Martian Depths" (*Wonder Stories*, 1933) might have been better suited to *Weird Tales*—but others are content to rejoice in their representations of the exotic. The best are those which deal with radical transfigurations of space and time, particularly "The Eternal World" (1932) and "The Dimension of Chance" (1932).

It is clear that Smith found some of these science-fictional tales impossible to take seriously, and some—like "Flight into Super-Time" (1932) and "The Monster of the Prophecy" (1932)—decay into uneasy satire. The seductive attraction of the exotic, however, was something which Smith was capable of taking very seriously indeed, and his best SF stories are pure celebrations of that allure. The most famous of them is "The City of the Singing Flame" (1931), which is combined in most book versions with its sequel "Beyond the Singing Flame" (1931).

The narrator of this story discovers on a lonely Californian ridge (effectively identical to the one where Smith lived) a gateway to a parallel world, where an assortment of alien creatures trek in pilgrimage to a fabulous city in order to achieve ecstatic immolation in a fountain of flame which attracts them with mesmeric music. Like some of the stories of A. Merritt (especially "The Moon Pool"), this story presents an archetypal image of the irresistible temptations of the imagination.

"Beyond the Singing Flame" is a much weaker story, and does the original no favors when combined with it, because the passage through the flame (which turns out to be a multidimensional gateway to other modes of existence) cannot help but be a de-mystification, and hence an anti-climax. The science-fictional imagination is inextricably involved with such de-mystifications and dis-enchantments, because it must deal in pretended possibilities. For this reason Smith could not find SF a satisfactory *genre* in which to work—the problem is just as obvious in "The Light from Beyond" (1934) as it is in "Beyond the Singing Flame"—but he was enthusiastic to borrow some elements of the science-fictional imagination, in order to add a more grandiose sweep to his fantasies. Two of his most gaudy and fanciful fantasies, "The Maze of the Enchanter" (1933) and "The Flower-Women" (1935), take advantage of an extraterrestrial setting to increase their exoticism.

It is hardly surprising, therefore, that Smith developed the most dramatically appropriate of all his imaginary *milieux* by placing it not in the remote past but in the farthest imaginable future. This was Zothique, "the world's last continent," in which decadence could be allowed unchallenged sway. The name may be derived from Rimbaud's *Album dit "Zutique,"* which title involves a fanciful piece of wordplay on the French expletive *zut!*—which might be parallelled (appropriately, if this is indeed where Smith got the name Zothique from) by some such English expression as "to hell with you!."

Because Hyperborea existed in earth's past, the viewpoint of the stories set there had to accept the implication that Order would ultimately oust Chaos, but in Zothique the implied future is empty; science and civilization are gone and utterly forgotten, and all that happens there is but part of a prelude to annihilation.

The first Zothique story was "The Empire of the Necromancers" (1932), a marvellous extravaganza in which two magicians conjure themselves an empire out of the dust of the ages and the corpses of the ancient dead, but then reap a just reward after the rebellion of their subjects. This is one of the most graphic of all Smith's horror stories, and its tone is pure nightmare:

> All that night, and during the blood-dark day that followed, by wavering torches or the light of the failing sun, an endless army of plague-eaten liches, of tattered skeletons, poured in a ghastly torrent through the streets of Yethlyreom and along the palace-hall where Hestaiyon stood guard above the slain necromancers. Unpausing, with vague, fixed eyes, they went on like driven shadows, to seek the subterranean vaults below the palace, to pass through the open door where Illeiro waited in the last vault, and then to wend downwards by a thousand steps to the verge of that gulf in which boiled the ebbing fires of earth. There, from the verge, they flung themselves to a second death and the clean annihilation of the bottomless flames.[8]

Not all the Zothique stories have this intensity of feeling. Some are ironic in the vein of the Hyperborean grotesques, most notably the excellent "The Voyage of King Euvoran" (1933), whose eponymous hero offends a necromancer and is punished by the loss of his remarkable crown, which is carried away by the re-animated fabulous bird that topped it. Misled by an apparently-favorable oracle, the king goes in quest of his lost crown, but finds instead a peculiarly apt humiliation.

Nor are all the Zothique stories entirely original—"The Isle of the Torturers" (1933) has echoes of Poe's "Masque of the Red Death" and Villiers de l'Isle-Adam's "Torture of Hope" embedded in its account of a sadistic orgy whose victim eventually wins a Pyrrhic victory over his tormentors. In general, though, the best of the Zothique stories are each possessed of an unparalleled dramatic surge which carries them helter-skelter through a mass of bizarre detail to a devastating conclusion.

The Zothique stories frequently contain erotic elements, but consummation is usually denied, and the seductive sorceresses who feature in "The Witchcraft of Ulua" (1934) and "The Death of Ilalotha" (1937) are certainly not treated with the same sentimental affection as the sorceresses and lamias of the tales of Averoigne—the Gautieresque touches of "The End of the Story," "The Holiness of Azédarac," and "The Enchantresss of Sylaire" (1941) are nowhere to be seen. Necrophilia is a theme which crops up several times, most strikingly in "The Death of Ilalotha" and "The Charnel God" (1934).

This repellent eroticism exists side-by-side with savage cruelty—torture is commonplace in Zothique and sadism is the norm. These quasi-pornographic features are not evidences of any depravity on the part of the author, but rather represent a determined effort to confront and make manageable the most nightmarish products of the imagination. Here, the most awful and terrifying creations of delirium and anxiety are submitted to the command of a rigorous literary imagination. The characters usually move in quasi-ritual step toward their predestined dooms, sometimes taking entire cities with them, as in "The Witchcraft of Ulua" and the very violent "The Dark Eidolon" (1935). The latter story, concerning a sorceror who defies his supernatural protector in order to carry forward his vendetta against a king who abused him in his youth, features a literal feast of horrors:

> In the wide intervals between the tables, the familiars of Namirrha and his other servants went to and fro incessantly, as if a fantasmagoria of ill dreams were embodied before the emperor. Kingly cadavers in robes of time-rotten brocade, with worms seething in their eye-pits, poured a blood-like wine into cups of the opalescent horn of unicorns. Lamias, trident-tailed, and four-breasted chimeras, came in with fuming platters lifted high by their brazen claws. Dog-headed devils, tongued with lolling flames, ran forward to offer themselves as ushers for the company. And before Zotulla and Obexah, there appeared

a curious being with the full-fleshed lower limbs and hips of a great black woman and the clean-picked bones of some titanic ape from there upward. And this monster signified by certain indescribable becks of its finger-bones that the emperor and his odalisque were to follow it.9

The background against which these stories are set is described in terms as far from naturalistic as the mechanics of their plots. Idiosyncrasy is displayed with unashamed extravagance, as in the opening paragraph of "The Witchcraft of Ulua":

> Sabmon the anchorite was famed no less for his piety than for his prophetic wisdom and knowledge of the dark art of sorcery. He had dwelt alone for two generations in a curious house on the rim of the northern desert of Tasuun: a house whose floor and walls were built from the large bones of dromedaries, and whose roof was a wattling composed of the smaller bones of wild dogs and men and hyenas. These ossuary relics, chosen for their whiteness and symmetry, were bound securely together with well-tanned thongs, and were joined and fitted with marvellous closeness, leaving no space for the blown sand to penetrate. This house was the pride of Sabmon, who swept it daily with a besom of mummy's hair, till it shone immaculate as polished ivory both within and without.10

In stories such as these the possibility of a happy ending is simply out of the question. For this reason they cannot be considered tragedies, or even simple horror stories, for no fate can really be considered tragic or horrific if it cannot possibly be avoided. Indeed, such is the inversion of values permitted by these stories that it is the echoes of affection and success which resound therein which seem in the end to be the most awful things of all. This can be seen in what are perhaps the finest of the tales of Zothique, "Necromancy in Naat" (1936) and "Xeethra" (1934).

In "Necromancy in Naat," a ship carrying a prince who is searching for his lost love (who has been carried off by slavers) is caught by a black current and wrecked near the island of Naat. The prince is the sole survivor, but finds himself reunited with the drowned crew of the ship—and with his loved one, also dead but reanimated—in the service of a family of necromancers, whose intention is to feed him to their vampiric familiar. He avoids this fate by joining in a plot to help the two sons murder their father, but in the hideous conflict which follows (in which the intended victim will not be still despite mortal wounds), he is killed. The sole surviving necromancer commits suicide, leaving the resurrected servants to find a "ghostly comfort" in their liberation:

> The quick despair that had racked him aforetime,
> and the long torments of desire and separation, were
> as things faded and forgot; and he shared with Dalili a
> shadowy love and a dim contentment.11

In "Xeethra," a goat-boy strays into the underworld realm of the dark god Thasaidon, where he eats fruit which recalls to him consciousness of a former existence as a king. He sets off to find his kingdom, but after a long journey finds it desolate and inhabited by lepers. He sells his soul to enter a dream in which the kingdom's lost glory is restored to him, agreeing to surrender it if ever he regrets his estate. Thasaidon eventually sends a dark piper to him in a time of strife, to seduce that all-important moment of regret. Xeethra becomes a goat-boy again, but the real horror of his fate is that Thasaidon does not need to snatch him away into some infernal region, because the anguish of his loss is hell enough for him, and the "dark empire" of Thasaidon is now within his soul.

It is in these images of special suffering, of death-in-life or hell-in-life, that Smith reaches the true culmination of all his trafficking with nightmares. In these two dénouements more than in any of his myriad tales which end with ugly death, he achieves a true moment of climax. If his quest into the farthest and strangest reaches of the imagination can be said to have reached a destination, this was surely it.

"Necromancy in Naat" was published two years after Smith's major phase of writing activity had petered out. Three more Zothique stories—"The Death of Ilalotha," "The Garden of Adompha" (1938), and "The Master of the Crabs" (1948)—were yet to appear, and a handful of other stories left over from the prolific phase filtered into print over the years, but Smith was never able to get back into the writing of prose on any significant scale. Those stories which seem to have been written at a much later date—"Schizoid Creator" (1953), "A Prophecy of Monsters" (1954), and "The Symposium of the Gorgon" (1958)—are brief literary jokes, manifesting none of the author's earlier fascinations.

This abrupt draining away of inspiration is in its way as remarkable as what his inspiration produced while Smith was possessed by it. It implies some essential change in Smith, whether in his personality or his environment. He offered no explanation himself, and was presumably unconscious of any reason.

One can only speculate about the possible psychodynamics of his literary endeavors and their frustrating conclusion, and such speculations are inevitably hazardous. Any conjecture remains untestable. There is, however, evidence in Smith's work of the motive force which carried him away to such far-flung fantasy worlds, and contemplation of this motive force does encourage certain hypotheses regarding possible reasons for its decline.

None of Smith's stories are in any straightforward sense autobiographical, but they do contain several pen-portraits of characters imbued with an escapist fervor which bears metaphorical comparison with his own. The writer Philip Hastane is a character who appears in several stories. He relays the manuscript which forms the story of "The City of the Singing Flame," and then becomes the protagonist of "Beyond the Singing Flame." He is also the narrator of two Lovecraftian tales: "The Hunters from Beyond" (1932), which is strongly reminiscent of Lovecraft's story, "Pickman's Model"; and "The Devotee of Evil" (1933).

In these stories it is not Hastane who is the focus of interest but the characters to whom things happen: the writer Giles Angarth, the sculptor Cyprian Sincaul, and the occultist Jean Averaud. Each of these three is seduced by the allure of the extraordinary into an encounter which destroys him (Angarth actually survives, but expresses the wish that he were dead). Averaud's fate is the most graphic—he builds a machine to put himself in touch with the ultimate evil, whose emanations apparently extend through all Creation, and is petrified by the possessive force of that evil. Although he is only a witness, Hastane too is touched and changed by this exposure:

> Vainly, through delirious months and madness-ridden years, I have tried to shake off the infrangible absession of my memories. But there is a fatal numbness in my brain, as if it too had been charred and blackened a little in that moment of overpowering nearness to the dark ray that came from pits beyond the universe. On my mind, as upon the face of the black statue that was Jean Averaud, the impress of awful and forbidden things has been set like an everlasting seal.[12]

To some extent, this must be seen simply as the kind of conclusion which a Lovecraftian story demands—the *genre* is characterized by its emphasis of the awfulness of moments of revelation which reveal the hideousness of the hidden order of the universe. But the lessons which Hastane learns from these encounters with men similar to himself seem to be accepted with real feeling.

Even in Smith's most romantic and sentimental stories, though there is nothing in *their* formula which demands it, there is nothing really to be gained from visionary experience. Among the least horrific of all Smith's stories is "The Planet of the Dead" (1932), which features a much more kindly vision, and a much more gentle visionary:

> By profession, Francis Melchior was a dealer in antiques; by avocation, he was an astronomer. Thus he contrived to placate, if not to satisfy, two needs of a somewhat complex and unusual temperament. Through his occupation, he gratified in a measure his his craving for all things that have been steeped in the mortuary shadows of dead ages, in the dusky amber flames of long-sunken suns; all things that have about them the irresoluble mystery of departed time. And through his avocation, he found a ready path to exotic realms in further space; to the only spheres where his fancy could dwell in freedom and his dreams could know contentment. For Melchior was one of those who were born with an immedicable distaste for all that is present or near at hand; one of those who have drunk too lightly of oblivion and have not wholly forgotten the transcendent glories of other eons, and the worlds from which they were exiled into human birth; so that their furtive, restless thoughts and dim, unquenchable longings return obscurely toward the vanishing shores of a lost heritage. The earth is too narrow for such, and the compass of mortal time is too brief; and paucity and barrenness are everywhere; and in all places their lot is a never-ending weariness.[13]

Melchior—whose situation is surely a fanciful transfiguration of Smith's own—shares for a while the consciousness of the poet Antarion, and his idyllic love affair with the lovely Thameera—a love affair brought to its conclusion by the death of the sun which lit their world. Though it is something to be treasured, Melchior's vision leaves him unhappier than ever, possessed by a "dull regret that he should ever have awakened."

These stories exemplify the most constant and oft-repeated pattern in Smith's work. No good ever really comes of dalliance with the supernatural. Very rarely is a character invigorated by it, and the exceptions belong to works in the flippant and satirical vein. The metempirical order of things is always either hostile or pregnant with doom. In most of his horror stories Smith's assumptions are very like those of H. P. Lovecraft or William Hope Hodgson, both of whom supposed that anything godlike must be implacably opposed to man, essentially evil. But Smith's version of this worldview does not concentrate on the evil nature of these hypothetical forces—even when, as in "The Devotee of Evil," such a case is made explicitly. His emphasis is on the utter irrelevance and insignificance of man, and the sheer help-lessness of human ambition in the face of cosmic processes which render human efforts meaningless and absurd. Thus, in "The Planet of the Dead" human affection is impotent in the face of cosmic catastrophe, just as in the Zothique stories *everything* is overshadowed by the impending end of earth. This sensibility is what links Smith to the Jansenist-influenced aspects of French Romanticism. Where can it have come from?

All Smith's notable fiction was written before the spring of 1934. His parents were then in their eighties, and both were soon to die. It seems highly probable that the problem of caring for them (in a lonely cabin with no electricity and no running water) became increasingly difficult, and that Smith was ultimately forced to stop writing largely because of the necessity of devoting his attention wholly to his parents' needs. His mother eventually died in September 1935 and his father in December 1937. One might expect that this would have freed him to begin writing again, but it did not, and this must surely make us wonder whether it was actually the situation of living with his aged parents, and the continually escalating strain which that situation put upon him, which is distortively reflected in his fantasies. The preoccupation with the inevitability of extinction, the idea that such inevitability made the longings of human affection impotent and absurd, and the constant emphasis on the sheer claustrophobia of real-world experience could all be linked in this way. If this is true, then the culmination of Smith's wilder stories in images of hell-in-life reflects no mere *ennui* or *spleen*, but rather a terrible anguish.

The memoirs written of Smith suggest that he was a very devoted son, and that he loved his parents dearly. If he was imprisoned on Boulder Ridge, it was by honest affection rather than by force. It is surely not too difficult to understand how the paradoxical character of such an imprisonment might lend itself well to expression in such paradoxical fantasies as Smith's. If the escapism of his fiction *is* to be seen as the "escape of the prisoner" rather than "the desertion of the soldier," then it was an escape which brought him very little in the way of consolation, perhaps because he was never quite able to see it that way himself. It might make more sense to see his creative burst of the early thirties not so much as an escape but as an expulsion, in which case his fantasy worlds were not so much places for him to visit as places into which he could pour the constructed phantoms of his resentments, his frustrations, and his fears—none of which would have been easy to accomodate or express in any other way. If one sees the creative period as a special purgation, then it may no longer be puzzling to ask why, once it was finished, it was finished for good.

To read and appreciate the work of Clark Ashton Smith requires more than a broad vocabulary and a sympathy for stylistic ornamentation. It requires the possibility of identifying with the curious worldview enshrined in that work: with a determination to get as far away from mundanity as language and the imagination can take one, and yet be content to discover there a universe utterly alien and inhumane, and to find in that revelation a sense of propriety which outweighs in value any mere comfort or pleasure. This may make Smith a difficult writer to enjoy, but it should not detract at all from the respect to which he is entitled.

An imagination which is bound by the aim of wish-fulfillment (as in so much romantic and heroic fantasy) could not begin to match Smith's achievement. Nor could an imagination narrowly directed to the production of the thrill of horror or disgust (as displayed in most horror stories). Smith's work is more exploratory in character, though it would not be confined, either, by the boundaries of scientific possibility which the science-fictional imagination respects. No other writer has been able to match him (including his own later self), not because none could master such an esoteric vocabulary or equal his teratological ingenuity, but because none has ever found that same combination of motive force and attitude, that same determined "alchemy of the word."

As with all true experiments in alchemy, Smith's literary work remains unique.

VII.

LITTLE VICTORIES

THE HEARTFELT FICTION OF PHILIP K. DICK

Since his death in 1982 Philip K. Dick has become established as a writer whose importance extends far beyond the boundaries of the science fiction genre. He was one of the most prolific contributors to the SF magazines during the boom of the 1950s, and to the paperback SF line edited by Donald A. Wollheim for Ace Books, where many of his early novels appeared as halves of Ace doubles. Until the last few years of his life such commercial and critical success as he gleaned was modest, but in recent years he has generated an enormous quantity of critical writing, becoming the most widely-praised and frenetically-analyzed SF writer of his or any other generation.

Dick's life has been described in detail in more than one biography, the most comprehensive being Lawrence Sutin's *Divine Invasions* (1989). The story told therein is that of a man afflicted with various discomfiting stress-related symptoms who never could adapt to the demands of ordinary social life. Born in 1928, he was unhappy and resentful as a child; he thought his mother unloving, and was inclined to charge her with having caused the death of his twin sister by neglect. He was prescribed amphetamines for the relief of his asthma and remained addicted to them for much of his life. He dropped out of college after a year and then held a few odd jobs, but even work in a record store proved too much to bear. He was married five times, but only two of the marriages were relatively long-lasting; he seems to have pursued relationships with (mostly very young) women with the same prolific obsessiveness he brought to his writing, as if he were compulsively in search of a relationship which might somehow constitute essential proof of his entitlement to full membership in the human race. The brief taste of fame which he achieved before his death served to intensify the maudlin anguish he felt about the many difficulties which afflicted his life, and to deepen the shade of the black humor which he employed to alleviate the intensity of his self-pity.

It is, of course, by no means unusual for social misfits to turn to writing as a vocation. The linked worlds of the Arts and Academia are the respectable refuges which modern society generously provides for those incapable of living a normal life, and literary work offers the most claustrophilic niche of all. Although modern critics are almost unanimous in claiming that Dick succeeded as a literary artist, turning his psychological difficulties to remarkable advantage as fuel for his vivid and marvellously off-beat imagination, it always seemed to him that his career was a catalogue of undeserved disappointments and the record of his published work a travesty of his true ambitions. He wanted to write "real" novels set in and passing judgment upon the real world—and he did, indeed, write a dozen of them—but the only things he could get into print were science fiction stories, about whose aesthetic merits he felt compelled to be defensive.

Only one of Dick's realistic novels saw print while he was alive, and that in a small press edition sixteen years after it was written. Most of the rest have since appeared, proving that even in his twenties he was a writer of ability, insight, originality, and courage—and proving also that a writer with all those things in his favor can be ignored by every single publisher in America. It did not help matters that Don Wollheim—the paymaster who provided the bulk of Dick's income for the greater part of his career—was by no means reluctant to advise him that he should give up trying to write mainstream fiction because he was no good at it. (Don Wollheim thought that almost all mainstream fiction was no good, especially literary fiction of a jaundiced complexion, and he was so entranced by science fiction himself that he simply could not imagine why anyone should be interested in writing anything else.)

The plot of one of the earliest as-yet-unpublished Dick novels, *Voices from the Street* (written 1952-53), is summarized by Sutin thus: "A young man, struggling with an unsatisfying job and a dreary marriage, falls into total despair when the supposed ideals of both politics and religion fail him." That might almost sum up Dick's entire canon of realistic fiction, except for the vital fact that his characters doggedly keep on struggling against such fates in their own ineptly courageous fashion, winning a host of little battles without ever coming within sight of victory in the war.

As a writer of science fiction novels, Dick was not allowed to reproduce that pattern in any straightforward fashion—not, at any rate, by Don Wollheim, who was a very firm believer in upbeat endings. (It was, of course, permissible to write short *contes cruels* with cleverly nasty-minded endings for the magazines, and Dick did so with relish.) Throughout his career Dick stirred restlessly and rebelliously beneath the yoke of these editorial expectations, compromising as best he could, but it was not until some years after *The Man in the High Castle* (1962) had won him a Hugo award, in spite of its gnomic ending, that he was able to work more brazenly towards resolutions which were essentially—if somewhat ironically—depressing. By this time he had become so adept at inflating the apparent value of little victories and looking aside from the loss of big wars that even his most horrific conclusions began to seem quite mild, if not strangely uplifting. It is a tribute to his remarkable gift for this paradoxical kind of prose that even the autobiographical essay which introduces his collection *The Golden Man* (1980)—which is surely the most grotesque hymn of whining self-pity ever penned—seems almost endearing.

Dick's first published work was "Beyond Lies the Wub," which appeared in *Planet Stories* in 1952. Humans exploring an alien world acquire a wub—a large piglike creature—with the intention of eating it, and will not be put off by its enthusiasm for discussing matters of metaphysics and moral philosophy; they find, however, that in spite of its meekness its outlook on life is uniquely adapted for survival. A later story, "Not by its Cover" (1968), credits the fur of the wub with the same deceptive power; the texts of books bound in it are neatly edited to embody the defiantly anti-atheistic wub philosophy of life.

Once he had made his first breakthrough Dick became a prolific producer of science fiction stories, which crept unostentatiously into the margins of the field. He could not sell to John W. Campbell Jr.'s *Astounding* because the ideological gulf between the two men was impossibly deep, but he was a fairly regular contributor to *The Magazine of Fantasy & Science Fiction* and *Galaxy*, and there were plenty of other markets to try until the end of the '50s, when the magazines died in droves.

The most memorable of Dick's early stories focus on the difficulty of distinguishing real individuals from *ersatz* imitations, as in tales of mechanical androids like "Impostor" (1953) and "Second Variety" (1953), or surreal tales like "The Father-Thing" (1954). This theme was, however, quickly magnified to take in more complex sets of appearances, as in the political fantasy "The Mold of Yancy" (1955), "The Unreconstructed M" (1956), and "A Glass of Darkness" (written 1953, published 1956, revised for book publication as *The Cosmic Puppets*, 1957); the last-named involves the deceptive transformation of a small town resulting from the active conflict between Good and Evil, here personified according to Zoroastrian mythology.

All these stories may be regarded as concretized extrapolations of paranoid suspicions, as may another set of stories in which seemingly innocent entities become dangerously hostile, including "Colony" (1953) and "Meddler" (1954). The mechanization of the environment and the computerization of political decision-making, which are luridly featured in the apocalyptic "Second Variety," also feature in a whole series of relatively long stories, which include "The Variable Man" (1953), "Autofac" (1955), and *Vulcan's Hammer* (1956; expanded for book publication 1960). Dick's attitude to highly-developed clever machinery is, however, far more complex than blanket suspicion or hostility. Intelligent machines sometimes feature in his early work in much

101

more benign roles, as in "The Last of the Masters" (1954), which features an altrustic robot.

These various continuing themes, and the attitudes enshrined therein, were to become greatly elaborated and exaggerated as Dick's career progressed. His accounts of what it would like to live in a world whose appearances are deceptive and whose inanimate components are becoming more active and mindful, and what strategies people might follow in adapting themselves to life in such a world, became increasingly thoughtful and increasingly desperate in tone.

Dick wrote his first full-length science fiction novel, *Solar Lottery* (1955; also known as *World of Chance*), in 1953-54, alongside the realistic novel *Mary and the Giant*. The latter was eventually published in 1987, in a version which Dick had revised—somewhat awkwardly, and, as it turned out, pointlessly—to editorial demand. In stark contrast to the calculatedly ground-breaking and controversial *Mary and the Giant*, *Solar Lottery* adopts the then-familiar framework of imagining a distorted future society corruptly dominated by some particular interest group and ripe for overthrow. It features such typically Dickian devices as an android assassin and a religious cult whose hopes for redemption are focused on a possibly-mythical tenth planet, but it is essentially an exercise in pastiche.

A similar attempt at conventional composition made at the same time was "Time Pawn" (1954; revised for book publication as *Dr. Futurity*, 1960), but it seems that Dick got lost in the convolutions of the plot—which he was presumably making up as he went along—and could not sort out the tangled threads even at the second attempt. This was to happen with increasing frequency, until he apparently decided that this problem too could be turned to peculiar advantage, and began to take delight in writing stories whose whole point was that no resolution of their intensively-recomplicated plots was possible or conceivable.

Presumably because *Mary and the Giant* failed to sell, in spite of his compromising revisions, Dick wrote several more SF novels before attempting another realistic one. *The World Jones Made* (1956) is more original and more impressive than its predecessor, following the career of a man with strictly limited precognition—who seems, to himself, to be living in a world which is lagging behind his own present by a year. His foreknowledge of a threatened "invasion" by enigmatic alien "drifters" allows him to whip up public anxiety and become a demagogue, but he remains impotent to change the world or his own fate. By concentrating on the endeavors of minor characters who are muddling through while this goes on, Dick avoids the bleak pessimism which would have saturated the story had he concentrated on its central character; he was to use the same strategy in many later novels written for Don Wollheim. *The Man Who Japed* (1956) follows the same formula as *Solar Lottery*, in a calculatedly irreverent fashion which is too slapdash to have much satirical bite. *Eye in the Sky* (1957), which was written earlier, is a much more significant novel which prefigures Dick's later work. A group of tourists caught in a freak accident are forced to live in a series of distorted worlds, each based in the beliefs of one of their number; in order to get back to reality the sane members of the group—who see the world as it really is—must expose the contradictions and illusions innate in the webs of false belief constructed by their fellows.

The next four novels which Dick wrote in 1955-57 were all realistic, presumably representing a concerted attempt to make up for the disappointing near miss he had suffered with *Mary and the Giant*. Two of them have since been lost; the others were the rather bizarre *The Broken Bubble* (1988) and *Puttering About in a Small Land* (1985). The last-named was certainly the best realistic novel which Dick had written to date, and is perhaps the best of the lot (although critical opinon is sharply divided on this point), but it failed to sell. Dick then attempted to blend the interests and techniques of his realistic fiction and science fiction together in *Nicholas and the Higs* and *Time out of Joint*. Although the first did not sell (and was subsequently lost), the second did, providing Dick with his first hardcover in 1959. It tells the story of Ragle Gumm, whose everyday life turns out to be a delusion occasioned by a psychotic withdrawal from reality, which is carefully maintained by military strategists exploiting his strange talent for anticipating bombing raids. Like the characters in *Eye in the Sky*, Gumm eventually recovers his true self and his grip on reality, but there are several awkward loose ends in the plot which cannot be accounted for within this schema.

While reworking a couple of magazine novellas into short novels for Ace, Dick returned to the writing of realistic novels in 1958-60, producing *In Milton Lumky Territory* (1985), *Confessions of a Crap Artist* (1975), *The Man Whose Teeth Were All Exactly Alike* (1984), and *Humpty Dumpty in Oakland* (1987). The last-named is a reworking of one of the lost novels of 1955-56, but the other three follow on from *Puttering About in a Small Land* in dealing with awkward moral dilemmas arising out of intimate relationships which are severely stressed by economic difficulties. Dick appears to have made a sustained effort to contrive uplifting endings for what are fundamentally downbeat stories, more than once employing the device of having a character who has previously shown no sign of extraordinary altruism rise to a particular challenge with courage and conviction. It made no difference; none of the novels sold at the time.

Following these disappointments Dick again went back to writing a kind of SF that made use of the methods he had by now brought to full maturity in his realistic fiction. *The Man in the High*

Castle (1961) was something of a breakthrough, winning the Hugo Award as best novel of its year (the first time that had been achieved by a novel which had not been serialized in one of the magazines). This surreal novel, in which the USA has been partitioned by the Germans and the Japanese following the total collapse of Europe in World War II, was not the first fantasy of its kind to contemplate the metaphysical implications of the notion of alternative worlds, but it was the first associated with genre SF. Dick used the *I Ching* as an oracular aid in composing the plot as well as a key device within the story; it reveals to the main character, Mr. Tagomi, that his world is not the "true" world, which is in fact contained within an alternative history novel written by one of the other characters (which describes a world more like, but not identical to, our own).

The *Man in the High Castle* came at the beginning of a decade which saw the rapid growth of a "counterculture" challenging all the established values of '50s America, and it caught the evolving mood very well. The rebellious and offbeat tendencies which had hitherto made Dick's work seem quirky and marginal now put him more in tune with the tide of fashion than any other SF writer. Recently embarked on his third marriage, with greater financial responsibilities than before, he set out purposefully to be a successful SF writer. The brilliant but relentlessly downbeat *We Can Build You* (1972), written in 1962, failed to find a publisher until it was serialized (as "A. Lincoln—Simulacrum" with a fake ending added by the magazine editor) in 1969, but the novels which followed contrived in various uplifting ways to ameliorate their own bleakness. Some of the more ambitious of them sold to better markets, while the remainder kept Don Wollheim's Ace line fully stocked. In 1962-65 Dick produced, in quick succession, *Martian Time-Slip* (Ballantine, 1964), *Dr. Bloodmoney* (1965), *The Game-Players of Titan* (1963), *The Simulacra* (1964), *Now Wait for Last Year* (Doubleday, 1966), *Clans of the Alphane Moon* (1964), *The Crack in Space* (1966), *The Three Stigmata of Palmer Eldritch* (1965), *The Zap Gun* (Pyramid, 1967), *The Penultimate Truth* (1964), *The Unteleported Man* (1966 in abridged form; 1983), *Counter-Clock World* (1967), and *The Ganymede Takeover* (1967, in collaboration with Ray Nelson).

Several of these novels cannibalized earlier short stories, and some must have been written—with the aid of amphetamines—in a matter of days, but even the undistinguished ones make effective use of what had by now become Dick's typical methods and central preoccupations. All of them deal in one way or another with distortions of reality by drugs, psychosis, alien intervention, or straightforward fraud. It is arguable that the best of the lot is *Martian Time-Slip*, written while he was still building up momentum, but the one which attracted most attention and praise was *The Three Stigmata of Palmer Eldritch*, whose main characters—like the protagonist of *Now Wait for Last Year*—become hopelessly and irredeemably trapped in webs of delusion which cannot be unravelled. Many of the novels are blatantly, if rather confusedly, misogynistic, reflecting the rapidly-escalating troubles into which Dick's current marriage had run.

At one point in 1963 Dick had his wife committed to a mental hospital for evaluation, although she had her own ideas about which of them was crazy, and subsequently persuaded her to take medication for supposed manic depression. Later that year Dick had a "vision" which became the seed of *The Three Stigmata of Palmer Eldritch* and led him to a brief flirtation with religious faith. Early in 1964 the marriage broke up; Dick never managed to set down roots again for more than a few months, and the confusion into which his life was cast was greatly enhanced by his association with the drug culture. It is astonishing that these upheavals did not immediately devastate his productivity, and doubly astonishing that he was able to mine his experiences to such effect that he was able to write two of his best books in 1966: *Do Androids Dream of Electric Sheep?* (1968) and *Ubik* (1969). These two books brought Dick's preoccupation with the relationship between real and *ersatz* entities and worlds to their highest level of complexity and intensity. In between the two he produced a juvenile SF novel which was eventually published as *Nick and the Glimmung* (1988).

Inevitably, though, Dick's output began to decelerate. His interest in the metaphysics of deception and delusion produced the neat comedy *Galactic Pot-Healer* (1969), which he later disparaged for making light of serious matters, although it is a better book than *A Maze of Death* (1970), which treats similar theological matters with unwarranted earnestness, or *Deus Irae* (1976), a planned collaboration that Roger Zelazny had to complete virtually unaided, which tries to do likewise but dissolves into confusion. *Our Friends from Frolix 8* (1970) is a thoroughly competent potboiler, but Dick's productivity ground to a juddering halt as he tried to complete the novel which ultimately became *Flow My Tears, the Policeman Said* (1974), another novel of drug-distorted reality apparently inspired by a mescaline trip. Three years passed before he was able to revise it. His fourth marriage broke up in 1970 and his already over-stressed life fell apart thereafter.

In the interim between the penultimate and final drafts of *Flow My Tears, the Policeman Said*, Dick opened his house to assorted drug abusers and juvenile delinquents, spent time in various mental hospitals, suffered a break-in concerning whose perpetrators he theorized wildly and endlessly, spent some time in Vancouver after being guest of honor at a convention there, and finally discovered another brief spell of stability with the teenage girl who became his fifth wife. When he had belatedly finished his novel-in-progress, he followed it up with another, even more intense, novel about drug-distorted reality based on his experiences of the three lost years, *A Scanner Darkly* (1977). He also wrote two of his most intense short stories, "A Little Something for us Tempunauts" (1973) and "The Pre-Persons" (1974), the latter a scathingly satirical anti-abortion story which drew wrathful responses from some of the field's newly-emergent feminists.

In stark contrast to Dick's early works, *A Scanner Darkly* took shape painfully slowly and was rewritten several times. Its progress was interrupted between the first and second drafts when he suffered (in February-March 1974) a new series of "visions," which were to obsess him for the remainder of his life and shape everything he wrote after *A Scanner Darkly*—which is justly regarded as a masterpiece by some critics, fusing as it does authentic experiences in highly dangerous territory with all the vigor and power of a brilliant and precisely-focused imagination. Dick never became certain whether his 1974 visions were inspired revelations, communications from some godlike entity, or delayed effects of the scrambling of his brain chemistry by amphetamines (which he had been forced to give up lest they kill him); it is perhaps inevitable that some of his admirers should prefer the first hypotheses, although the last is infinitely more likely.

It is not at all surprising that Dick should have used these visionary experiences in his fiction, nor is it altogether surprising that he should do so in a manner which suggested that he—like so many of his characters—had so comprehensively lost his grip on reality as never to be able to recover it. Even so, the novel whose first draft (written in 1976) was eventually issued as *Radio Free Albemuth* (1985) and whose second version (written in 1978) was published as *VALIS* (1981) is as vivid and as readable as his earlier works. Its "sequel," *The Divine Invasion* (1981), is handicapped by a certain *recherché* quality (derived from the wide-ranging reading he did in attempting to comprehend and come to terms with his visionary experiences), and might not, in the final analysis, make any sense at all, but Dick had long since defused and disarmed critical complaints of that nature. Ironically, *The Transmigration of Timothy Archer* (1981)—the only realistic novel Dick had ever been commissioned to write, turned out to be far from realistic. Dick remained, however, a writer capable of considerable elegance and more-than-considerable force. His short story "Frozen Journey" (1980; better known as "I Hope I Shall Arrive Soon") retains all the simplicity and clarity of his very best work in that medium.

It can now be understood that the awesome posthumous success which Dick has enjoyed arose from a fortuitous combination of his particular interests and abilities and the circumstances which provided their context.

Dick came to prominence in a period when science fiction expanded rapidly out of its magazine ghetto into the much wider world of popular culture. There, John W. Campbell Jr.'s insistence that real SF was based in the conscientious extrapolation of actual science not only cut no ice, but came to seem like an eccentric handicapping system designed to detract from the comprehensibility and easy narrative flow of SF. Authors like Dick, who deployed imaginary technologies without the least regard for nitpicking matters of rational plausibility, suddenly found that they were no longer condemned to marginality, but could in fact bid to create a new core and center for the field.

Dick had caught the leading wave of the '60s counterculture, and he was just as nicely placed in the '80s to catch the attention of new movements in literary criticism which became intently interested in the problematic relationships between the imaginary worlds within texts and "reality." As academic questions about the meanings and interrelationships of literary texts became murkier, Dick's relentless fascination with deceptive appearances, and his unashamed abandonment of any commitment to restore coherency to his plots, came to seem even more daring and much more pertinent than he probably intended.

Above all else, though, it was the sheer *fervor* of Dick's work which commanded attention; no other writer got quite as excited about his imaginative materials, or compelled the reader to become intimately involved in the strange situations in which his characters find themselves. He was able to care deeply about dilemmas which no one had ever bothered to care about before, and he was able to make his readers care about them too. It goes without saying that no one who is capable of living a normal life is likely to be able to do this, but it is worth noting that most people who are incapable of living a normal life cannot do it either. Dick's success as a writer undoubtedly owed something to his failure to become a well-adjusted social being, but that makes it all the more remarkable that he was able to produce such amazingly rich and delicately-woven fabulations.

VIII.

GERNSBACK'S PESSIMIST

The Futuristic Fantasies of David H. Keller

David H. Keller was already middle-aged when his wife showed him a copy of Hugo Gernsback's newly-founded *Amazing Stories* in 1926 and suggested that he might try to write for it. Gernsback was so enamored of Keller's first submission, "The Revolt of the Pedestrians"—which he published in 1928—that he immediately offered a commission for a dozen more stories at the unusually generous rate of $60 apiece.

Keller promptly became Gernsback's most prolific contributor, publishing a veritable flood of stories in 1928 and 1929, under the spur of a period of financial hardship which forced him briefly to rely on his pen for a living. He quickly branched out into the writing of articles on psychoanalysis for a periodical run by Gernsback's brother Sidney, horror stories for *Weird Tales*, and mundane fiction for *Ten Story Book* (where it appeared under the byline Amy Worth). His productivity declined steadily thereafter, and he published very little science fiction once Gernsback had left the scene, but he made a crucial contribution to the early development of the *genre*. He was the first author of original material to be widely featured in the specialist pulps, and his early stories made a deep impression on many of their readers.

Most of the new authors recruited to Gernsback's cause were young men whose imaginations had been fired by the pulps, but the most significant writers of the late '20s and early '30s were mature men who had been writing imaginative fiction for some time without being able to find an appropriate market: Keller, Stanton A. Coblentz, John Taine, and Stanley G. Weinbaum. Keller was the oldest of these, having been born in 1880 in Philadelphia.

In his infancy Keller had extraordinary difficulty in learning to make himself understood verbally, and had to be placed in a remedial school until he was nine. Because language was something which he had been forced to acquire by artifice rather than by nature—as other people seemed to do—it remained an object of special fascination to him; he became a prolific writer for his own private purposes. The chief legacy of this fascination was a curiously painstaking and seemingly naïve literary style, which gave many of his stories an eccentric fabular quality. He used his own experiences as the seed of the intriguing SF story, "The Lost Language" (1934).

After transferring to grammar school Keller quickly made up lost ground and overtook his contemporaries. He began writing fiction and poetry at fourteen, and was ambitious to follow an academic career, but his father would not finance his studies unless they were aimed towards a conventional profession, so he entered Medical School. While there he published several stories in amateur publications, including several—under the pseudonym Henry Cecil—in *The White Owl*, a periodical imitative of the influential "little magazine" *The Black Cat*. *The Black Cat*, which published Jack London's first story and several notable fantasies, owed its own inspiration to the literary magazines of Paris; *Le chat noir* had been the periodical which launched the Decadent Movement.

Keller eventually became a "horse-and-buggy doctor" in a small town in Pennsylvania, but that position came to an end in 1914, after which he held a number of equally unhappy short-term appointments before serving in the Medical Corps when America became involved in World War I. From 1919-29 he worked in a state hospital in Pineville, Louisiana, but quit in disgust when Huey Long was elected governor (it was this move which required him to live for a while on the proceeds of his writing). Keller had been writing prolifically throughout his time at Pineville, producing numerous novels and novellas—some of which were to form the basis of published work in a later phase of his career—but publishing only a history of his family, *The Kellers of Hamilton Township* (1922), and a volume of poetry signed Henry Cecil. Cecil was a surname borrowed from a branch of his family, which is frequently attached to characters in his fiction; Hubler was another name likewise associated with some of his ancestors and routinely attached to his fictional alter egos.

After briefly holding other posts, Keller settled down again in the state hospital for the feeble-minded at Pennhurst, Pennsylvania, remaining there for nearly five years. He then returned to his "ancestral home" in Monroe County, a house named Underwood, with the intention of devoting himself to literary work for the rest of his life. He still held a commission in the Medical Reserve, though, and he was recalled to active duty as a teacher at the Army Chaplain's School in 1941, remaining there until his retirement in 1945. His retirement was followed by a renewal of his literary activity, but he hardly ever bothered to submit his work for publication. His "professional career," such as it was, continued with the reissuing of much of his pulp fiction by reprint magazines and the small presses specializing in SF, but most of the work which appeared for the first time in this period had been written much earlier. He continued writing until he died in 1966, but very little of his later work saw print in any form.

It is easy enough to understand why Hugo Gernsback was keen to enlist Keller in the ranks of *Amazing*'s contributors. He was a man of the same generation (Gernsback was four years younger than he), his medical degree lent a welcome aura of authority to his work, and that work displayed—to begin with, at least—a vivid inventiveness. The views of the two men were, however, markedly different. Keller had nothing like the extravagant enthusiasm for the coming "Atom-Electronic Age" that Gernsback professed and was ambitious to promote. Keller's science fiction mostly consists of cautionary tales which warn that rapid and reckless technological advance has the potential to reduce or obliterate the quality of human life. The methods he used in making this point were unashamedly melodramatic, often visiting death and destruction on a massive scale upon those characters foolish enough to be seduced by their technology. In "The Revolt of the Pedestrians," a ruling caste of automobilists whose lower limbs have atrophied through long disuse is casually condemned to extinction by the lower orders whose rights they stubbornly refuse to recognize.

Keller was no simple-minded reactionary opposed to any and all technological progress, but he did have a marked Luddite streak. He was deeply anxious about the particular ways in which technology was being applied in contemporary society, within the economic context provided by Industrial Capitalism. One of the most graphic of his early stories was "Stenographer's Hands" (1928), in which an industrial magnate embarks upon a program of selective breeding in order to produce individuals uniquely adapted for secretarial work. Unfortunately, the development of adept fingers and a docile temperament is correlated with a more general deterioration which results in a race of "degenerate epileptics."

Exactly what Keller's political views were remains unclear—his reaction to Long's election and his SF both offer much clearer evidence of what he was against than of what he was for—but he certainly had strong feelings about contemporary trends towards "degeneracy," and he was firmly attached to the notion that contemporary civilization was in some way "sick." In his fiction, at least, he was perfectly happy to contemplate Draconian attempts to cure this sickness—a willingness which makes some of his stories monstrously offensive to the modern eye. His occasionally-rampant racism and his seemingly-firm belief in negative eugenics are given lavish expression in the four-part tale "The Menace" (1928). In this story-sequence negroes who contrive to turn themelves white are summarily dealt with, and its climax features the extermination of all "insane" individuals—who constitute, by this time, more than 99% of the population, because living under glass has denied virtually everyone the sanity-promoting effects of direct sunlight. "The Yeast Men" (1928), which describes a bizarre kind of biological warfare, features a similarly drastic winnowing process.

Keller also wrote tales of future domestic life, which are much less melodramatic but are equally uninhibited in their own fashion. Most of his stories in this vein exhibit an extraordinarily indulgent sentimentality. "A Biological Experiment" (1928) tells the story of a couple who rediscover the joys of natural parenthood in a world where the standard method of reproduction is ectogenetic. In "Unlocking the Past" (1928), a mother refuses to allow her child to participate in an experiment to revive ancestral memories when a dream reminds her of the likely unpleasantness of such memories. In "The Psychophonic Nurse" (1928), a mother belatedly realizes that she and her child are both suffering deprivation by virtue of her use of a mechanical nanny.

All these stories are innocent of any literary sophistication, but those which deal with biotechnology—as almost all Keller's work in this vein does to some degree—constitute a fascinating discourse on topics raised by J. B. S. Haldane in his classic futurological essay, *Daedalus; or, Science and the Future* (1923). Keller had almost certainly read this essay—as, of course, had Aldous Huxley, whose own alarmist ruminations on the themes thereof were later to be embodied in *Brave New World* (1932). Keller's anxieties about the human cost which might have to be paid for technological advancement are, however, most heartfeltly summed up in a vivid dream-sequence in "The Threat of the Robot" (1929), whose protagonist foresees automation causing mass unemployment:

> In those dreams Ball saw the gradual starvation of society, first, for the real pleasures of life, then for the comforts, and later on for the actual necessities. He visioned parades of unemployed workingmen, demanding of capital a right to earn a living. But these very parades were policed by robots with blue-coats on who were very perfect in preserving order by mechanically-wielded batons. In his dream, Ball saw one strike a poor woman on the head. The baby that she carried dropped out of her lifeless arms and would have fallen to the pavement, but Ball caught it with one hand and struck the robot in the face with the other. At once he was the center of an attack from a dozen machines who pounded him into insensibility. As he fell, he tried to save the child, crying in his terror, "You are killing civilization, instead of the man."
>
> But instead of hitting the concrete, he floated into the air, and the child turned into a football. Seeing that he had on the old football armor of former days, he plunged madly through the gathering clouds to make a touchdown. Helping him were two of his former friends who had died. They whispered to him

that he could save the world from electrified machinery if he only wanted to.[1]

In his first novel, *The Human Termites* (1929; reprinted as a chapbook in 1979), Keller imagined human nations as primitive "hive-minds" which are perceived as an emergent threat by the ancient hive-minds of the social insect species. The insects move to exterminate these upstart rivals, creating monstrous semi-human termites to serve as their armies. These co-opt, enslave, and destroy the greater part of the human species before they are ultimately thwarted.

By this time, however, the highly-productive Keller was clearly running out of imaginative inspiration, and his work was beginning to seem tiredly repetitive. Another exercise in horrific giantism was "The Worm" (1929), an oddly effective story loaded with presumably-conscious symbolism in which a man living alone in an old mill struggles to preserve the edifice against the depredations of the horror gnawing away at its foundations. Subsequently, however, his stories of giant insects decayed into vapid silliness, as exemplified by "The Flying Threat" (1930) and "The Solitary Hunters" (1934).

Mass unemployment threatens yet again in "White Collars" (1929), this time affecting the professional classes because of the over-production of college graduates. "The Feminine Metamorphosis" (1929) is a spectacularly nasty-minded exercise in unabashed male chauvinism and vicious racism, in much the same vein as "The Menace," to which it as a sequel of sorts. Here, women who employ a chemical method of masculinization in order to compete in a male-dominated world discover that all the Chinamen who have been castrated *en masse* to provide their supplies of testosterone are infected with a horrible disease (which is coyly left unnamed, but is obviously syphilis).

Keller's second and third novels, "The Conquerors" (1929) and "The Evening Star" (1930), are sadly stereotyped exercises in pulp melodrama, the second being his only venture into interplanetary fantasy. Both seem to be straightforwardly derivative of other stories he had encountered in the pulps. The distinctive outlook and method of his earlier works continued to show in a small minority of his shorter stories, including "Free as the Air" (1931), in which entrepreneurs subject atmospheric oxygen to the logic of the marketplace, and "No More Tomorrows" (1932), about the effects of a curious elixir of life of dubious authenticity.

It was not until Keller's production schedule relaxed considerably that he was able to revert to more distinctive work. His fourth novel, "The Metal Doom" (1932), is easily the best of his pulp serials. It is a disaster story in which all metals are stricken by unnaturally rapid corrosion, forcing humanity to revert to Stone Age technologies. At the end of the story the main characters reflect on the lessons learned from their bitter experiences, and conclude that the collapse of their allegedly diseased civilization was after all a good and necessary thing. This recognition is swiftly followed by a *deus ex machina* which restores the metals so that the chastened human race might have a second chance.

Keller's next novel, "Life Everlasting" (1934; reprinted in *Life Everlasting and Other Tales of Fantasy and Horror*, 1947) adds a curious twist to this notion of a sick civilization. Here the world is transformed in a very different way by the discovery of a panacea which offers perfect physical, mental, and moral health to everyone, in perpetuity, imposing only one compensating penalty by virtue of rendering its eternally-youthful immortals sterile. The loss of the pleasures of parenthood proves so difficult to bear, however, that the discoverer of the panacea is urged to develop an antiserum. The author neglects to inform the reader as to whether this "cure" returns deviance and immorality to the world along with disease and deformity, and refrains from explaining why people could not simply have their children before using the immortality serum.

Keller was to become increasingly interested in the "chemistry of morality," which is a minor theme in "Life Everlasting." "The Tree of Life" (1934) features a drug which obliterates the moral inhibitions of the inhabitants of a village—a thought-experiment repeated on a larger scale in the most interesting of his later works, the novella "The Abyss," which was sufficently shocking to preclude publication in a magazine medium dominated by strict taboos, and eventually appeared in the private press book *The Solitary Hunters and the Abyss* (1948).

Keller's most effective work of the mid- and late thirties consisted of psychological horror stories and *contes cruels*, including the oft-reprinted "The Thing in the Cellar" (1932), in which a parent's attempt to prove to his child that there is no monster in the cellar by locking him in goes tragically awry. (The plot of the story has been frequently reproduced, presumably by independent inspiration.) "The Literary Corkscrew" (1934), in which a man whose creativity is linked to pain is equipped with a device which keeps his work conveniently up to standard, is similarly graphic. One of his "Amy Worth" stories, "A Piece of Linoleum" (1933) is a startling study of unthinking callousness, while "The Dead Woman" (1933)—in which a man becomes convinced that his wife is dead and kills her in consequence—proved too strong for the editors of the day and had to be given away to a fanzine (although it was reprinted in a pulp magazine in 1939). "The Doorbell" (1934) is another nasty-minded tale involving capsules containing fishhooks and a powerful magnet.

With Gernsback gradually moving out of the picture Keller seems to have had much greater difficulty finding markets for his science fiction in this period. "Unto Us a Child Is Born" (1933) is a moving story about the downside of positive eugenics, tracking the experiences of two gifted parents commissioned to produce a very special child, but the very similar "The Mother" proved unsalable and eventually appeared in a fan magazine in 1938.

Among the contacts which Keller made in the fan community was Régis Messac, then working as a college teacher in Montréal. When Messac returned to France he helped found a periodical called *Les Primaires*, for which he began translating some of Keller's work. Messac published a booklet of three translated pulp SF stories in 1936 and subsequently began issuing some of Keller's earlier works, including the novella which was eventually to see US publication as *The Eternal Conflict* (1939 in French; 1949 in English) and four linked short stories, *The Sign of the Burning Hart* (1938; reprinted 1948). *The Eternal Conflict* is a remarkable allegorical fantasy based in the theories of Sigmund Freud, elaborately displaying the supposed symbolism of dreams in an attempted analysis of female psychology.

Encouraged by Messac's interest, Keller rewrote two of his other early novellas as the novel *The Devil and the Doctor* (1940), an exercise in literary Satanism clearly inspired by two of his favorite authors, Anatole France and James Branch Cabell. Keller later recalled that Simon & Schuster, publishers of *The Devil and the Doctor*, seemed to repent of their decision and refused to take booksellers' orders long before remaindering their stock, perhaps because of pressure from religious groups who found the novel's portrayal of Satan as an urbane friend of mankind insufferable. It may have been this unhappy experience which caused Keller to revert almot exclusively to amateur status, never thereafter seeking mass-market publication for his work. A second exercise in literary Satanism, *The Homunculus* (1949), was eventually issued by the Prime Press, although the identity of the Devil is delicately obscured, presumably for diplomatic reasons. Another early novella, *The Lady Decides* (1949)—a curious Quixotic romance in which one Henry Cecil embarks on an allegorical odyssey in Spain— was subsequently issued by the Prime Press as a companion to *The Eternal Conflict*.

Keller's last significant science fiction story was "The Abyss," which was presumably the story he was referring to when he wrote a memoir of his life for *Fantasy Commentator* in 1947, saying "I am working on a novel centering around an idea that as far as I know is absolutely new to modern literature." It describes the events which follow the heavily-advertised marketing by an experimentally-inclined industrialist of drugged chewing-gum to the inhabitants of New York City. As a result, the repressive legacy of two thousand years of civilization is stripped away, letting loose the rapacious appetites of the id. Although the theory supporting the plot is basically Freudian, Keller makes explicit use of the ideas of Carl Jung in planning the grotesque imagery of the story. There is a political gloss which suggests that charismatic dictators like Nero and Hitler work in a not-dissimilar fashion to mobilize and channel the worst impulses of their subjects, but the real point of the story is the insistence that repression is a necessary and thoroughly good thing, and that the veneer of civilization covers a deep and terrible psychic abyss.

At first sight this message may seem to contrast sharply with that of "The Metal Doom," where civilization has to be destroyed before it can be reconstructed along more reasonable lines, but there is no ideological conflict between the two stories. The surreal fantasy "The God Wheel"—which was presumably written in the same period as "The Abyss," appearing for the first time in Keller's second story collection *Tales from Underwood* (1952)—reiterates the theme of cleansing the world by restoring Arcadian innocence. The apocalyptic violence celebrated here and so frequently unleashed in Keller's SF stories always erupts because the veneer of civilization has been brought to breaking-point by unbearable stress; the author is always steadfast in support of what he considers the truly fundamental and absolutely necessary elements of "civilization": marital and parental love, respect for the rights of others, and a sort of polite tolerance (which unfortunately did not extend to matters of race and sex).

Few readers would consider these unworthy objectives, as far as they go, and it is arguable that the oddest thing about Keller's work is that he should consider it necessary to go to such extreme imaginative lengths in championing such widely-accepted ideals. He works so very hard to achieve this end, and sometimes finds himself driven to such absurd lengths (as in "Life Everlasting") in order to make his point, that one can hardly help suspecting him of protesting a little too much. His commercial work—which includes almost all his SF—has not quite the same intensely personal quality as those stories which are populated by lightly-disguised and steadfastly-eccentric avatars of himself (*The Devil and the Doctor*, *The Homunculus*, and *The Lady Decides* are obvious examples), but it is at least possible that it gives plainer voice to the anxieties which haunted him. His many tales of marital disharmony and parental dissatisfaction, almost all of which are brought to sickly sweet but exaggeratedly-contrived conclusions—"The Golden Bough" (1935) is a telling exception—may be more revealing than he intended. Given his training and long experience in psychiatric medicine, he must have been fully aware of the sexual symbolism which appears in many of the stories which he claimed to have derived from dreams or to have written under "self-hypnosis" at the behest of his subconscious, and this might well have made him hypersensitively wary of the sinister side of his own repressed impulses.

David H. Keller is not quite forgotten today, although the last hardcover collection of his tales, *The Folsom Flint and Other Curious Tales*, was issued in 1969, and it now seems unlikely that any more of his many unpublished novels will see the light. Some of his uncollected pulp stories were reprinted in the late 1960s during the period when *Amazing Stories* became part of a chain of reprint magazines cannibalizing the legacy of its earlier incarnations. Patrick and Dixie Adkins's P.D.A. Enterprises began issuing "The David H. Keller Memorial Library" in 1978, but it only extended to two volumes before the project collapsed. It is, therefore, extremely difficult for the modern reader to gauge the extent of Keller's contribution to the early evolution of pulp SF, which was considerable and perhaps crucial.

Keller was the first writer to dabble extensively in stories of future biotechnology and to insist that the new ethical problems which would inevitably arise in connection with such technologies would be very awkward indeed. He wrote stories whose explicit moral was that marvellous inventions were worthless unless they supported and sustained—or at least did not disrupt—the intimate personal relationships which are the warp and weft of human society. He helped to provide a useful counterweight to the extravagant adventure stories which were to become the staple diet of the SF pulps by writing stories calculated to disturb, and by posing questions about the social role of technology which more technophilic writers were thereby forced to address.

The style which Keller employed for his science fiction was excruciatingly crude, and cannot pass therein—as it can and does in much of his other work—for calculatedly naive charm. This is partly due to the fact that pulp SF writers in general had not yet contrived to standardize a vocabulary of images and a narrative method which would permit the construction of imaginary worlds without recourse to massively cumbersome info-dumping, but it testifies to his own inability to make significant headway in coping with such problems. It would, however, be a pity if this failure were to condemn his science fiction to remain unread while his supernatural fiction continues to command a certain esoteric respect. Perhaps it is only of antiquarian interest, and it certainly requires to be read with an understanding of its historical context, but it was both striking and challenging in its day, and the Gernsback magazines would have been poorer without it.

IX.

SCHEMES OF SALVATION

THE LITERARY EXPLORATIONS OF THEODORE STURGEON

Theodore Sturgeon joined John W. Campbell Jr.'s stable of science fiction writers in 1939, and he was still working in the years immediately prior to his death in 1985, but almost all the fiction for which he is remembered was written between 1946 and 1962. He spent the last twenty years of his life suffering from a "writer's block" which he breached only occasionally and without ever recovering the power of his early work; the Hugo and Nebula awards given to "Slow Sculpture" in 1970 were a belated recognition of his contribution to the history of the genre rather than testimony to the merits of that particular story.

Sturgeon's motto in his later years was "Ask the next question!"; he was fond of arguing that if and when people stopped doing that they were effectively dead, and he was wont to declare that resistance to change is "the only unnatural practice." The fact that he found it impossible to make further progress in his own creative endeavors must have been exceedingly frustrating, but he was no stranger to frustration. Indeed, the great majority of his memorable works may be regarded as elaborate studies of extraordinarily extreme frustration, sometimes—but by no means always—magically redeemed in an equally extreme fashion.

Theodore Sturgeon was an adopted name, the surname being that of his stepfather (his difficult relationship with his stepfather is featured in *Argyll, a Memoir*, 1993, a chapbook essay discovered among his posthumous papers). He was born Edward Hamilton Waldo in New York City in 1918. Initially rather puny, he was spurred on by his tough-minded stepfather to become a gymnast of considerable prowess, but his dreams of making a career as an acrobat were dashed by a severe bout of rheumatic fever when he was fifteen. When he recovered his health, he went to nautical college to train as an officer, but after resolutely enduring the routine bullying for a year, he settled for life as an ordinary seaman.

While at sea Sturgeon began writing short fiction for a newspaper syndicate, eventually returning to shore in the hope of building a career on the shaky foundation of what were then very meager returns.

After seeing a copy of the first issue of *Unknown* in 1939 he began sending stories to John Campbell. His earliest submission, "Helix the Cat," failed to sell until it appeared in the Campbell Memorial Anthology, *Astounding* (1973), edited by Harry Harrison, but he soon made his debut in *Astounding* with "Ether Breather" (1939), quickly followed in *Unknown* by "A God in a Garden" (1939), which had been written earlier.

Sturgeon's interests and writing style were much better suited to *Unknown* than *Astounding*. "Ether Breather" and its sequel are light, humorous pieces which could counterbalance the more earnest material which Campbell was trying to bring to a new level of sophistication, but Sturgeon could not adapt himself to the kind of "hard SF" which was the magazine's staple diet. Campbell must have fed him the plot for "Artnan Process" (1941)—a space opera whose plot turns on an esoteric problem in isotope separation—but Sturgeon obviously found the composition of the story awkward and uncongenial. His imaginatively-unfettered work for *Unknown* was much more exuberant and occasionally brilliant, ranging from delightfully quirky comedies through neat *contes cruels* to the vividly horrific "It" (1940), which features a kind of ultimate monster: the distilled essence of teratology.

Sturgeon did, however, make one contribution to *Astounding* which made a deep impression on its readers, even though he did not like the story himself. This was "Microcosmic God" (1941), in which a scientist takes advantage of the technological products of a miniature world where time runs at a much faster rate than in our own, until the tiny "Neoterics" invent a force-shield with which to isolate themselves from further interference. The readers who elevated this story to classic status were presumably impressed by the central motif of the artificial world, but Sturgeon was never much interested in ideas for their own sake; for him "Microcosmic God" was a parable of cynical exploitation fostering megalomania, which unfortunately failed to reach a morally-satisfying conclusion. The last line of the story is of a kind which always appealed to Campbell, but it is quite foreign to the intimately personal conclusions which Sturgeon favored. Sturgeon's true strength as a writer was an ability to get inside his characters, to explore and pass judgment on the fundamental wellsprings of their motivation: their inmost impulses and desires; their most jealously-guarded secrets.

As an adept student of human behavior Sturgeon was very conscious of the cruelty which lurked beneath the masks of civilization, and the ways in which the taboos of conventional morality (which he was always careful to distinguish from more fundamental ethical systems) could pervert even healthy and benevolent sentiments into anxieties and phobias. Readers who found him uncomfortable—as did the many American editors who rejected his horror story "Bianca's Hands" before it won a competition run by the British *Argosy* in 1947—accused him of having a "nasty mind," but in fact he had a mind so abundantly stocked with the "rebel passions" pity and anguish that he could not help reacting with naked horror to the nastiness he perceived in others. "Microcosmic God" did not seem to him to be one of his better stories precisely because it was deflected away from its study of the conscienceless exploitation of the Neoterics by their tyrant-God to a more objective consideration of the longer-term implications of the story's central premise. This broadening of imaginative horizons was a primary concern of Campbellian science fiction, but for Sturgeon science-fictional ideas were potentially-ingenious instruments for use in the construction of parables regarding the human condition and the ills afflicting it.

Given this, it is not surprising that Sturgeon found it increasingly difficult to cope with Campbell's editorial demands. By the time "Microcosmic God" appeared in print he had effectively abandoned writing, and he spent the next five years doing various odd jobs to earn a living. During this interim he produced only one SF story: the novella "Killdozer!" (1944), in which an archetypal product of modern technology is arbitrarily invaded by an alien force which sets forth to annihilate everything human from its surroundings. Campbell—who presumably, and perhaps quite rightly, never paused to wonder whether this might be an oblique caricature of his own ideals—gratefully published it at a time when his sources of material had been severely depleted by the effects of the war.

When Sturgeon began writing again, he produced some striking cautionary tales inspired by the advent of the atom bomb, including "Memorial" (1946) and "Thunder and Roses" (1947), and some heartfelt stories of first contact between humans and aliens in which communication proves tragically difficult to establish, including "Mewhu's Jet" (1946) and "Tiny and the Monster" (1947). The most powerful, and perhaps the most revealing, of the early stories of this new phase was the novella "Maturity" (1947), which tracks a female doctor's frustrating relationship with a childlike man who is psychologically blocked in the quest to develop his extraordinary creative gifts. Her determination to bring him to what she considers to be maturity is ultimately fruitless, but he claims to have found an infinitely more modest maturity of his own definition.

The depth of feeling in "Maturity" is remarkable, and was quite unprecedented in pulp science fiction. Sturgeon went on to explore many more ways of allegorizing the alienation and and frustration of sensitive individuals, but he had difficulty finding appropriate markets for such work despite the high regard which editors had for his talents. He published extensively in *Weird Tales*, placed his first novel and several novelettes in *Fantastic Adventures*, and was not ashamed to deploy the lushly colorful imagery of *Planet Stories* in "The Incubi of Parallel X" (1951), but it was the founding of *Galaxy* in 1950 which offered him the opportunity to forge a niche tailored to his own requirements.

After 1949 Sturgeon made only one more apppearance in Campbell's *Astounding* with the slyly non-serious "Won't You Walk—?" (1956). This parting of the ways is all the more significant when one bears in mind that in this period Campbell and Sturgeon both became intensively preoccupied with the notion of "*psi*-powers": telepathy, psychokinesis, precognition, etc.

Belief in such strange powers of the mind was very old, and they had long been featured in imaginative fiction of all kinds, but it was not until J. B. Rhine of Duke University provided them with a new pseudoscientific jargon and an alleged basis in statistical abormalities derived from laboratory experiments that they attained a mask of respectability adequate to earn them a leading role in *Astounding Science Fiction*. Campbell became conviced that the phenomena recorded by Rhine and his followers were evidence that a giant leap in human evolution was already in the making, and *Astounding* pushed this notion as hard as it had earlier pushed the (now vindicated) notion that atomic power would soon become a reality. The moral implications of this development were by no means neglected, and stories of unjustly persecuted supermen were commonplace in *Astounding*. Campbell's conception of the moral questions at stake was admirably summed up in the Hugo-winning serial *They'd Rather Be Right* (1954) by Mark Clifton and Frank Riley, whose concluding monologue is pure Campbell, arguing that people must give up their entrenched prejudices and overcome their conservative fears if they are to take advantage of new technologies and new mental powers.

At first sight, Sturgeon's interest in *psi*-powers appears very similar to Campbell's. He too was fond of writing tales of unjust persecution whose message was that people ought to abandon their entrenched prejudices, and he too became fascinated with the imagery of a sudden transcendent evolutionary leap. In fact, though, the two men approached the problem from opposite directions and the fiction they favored carried a very different thrust. Campbell's approach modelled that of the scientist: here is the fact of emergent *psi*-powers, what are the logical consequences? For Sturgeon, the primary fact was that of the deeply frustrating sense of alienation possessed by all people who felt themselves to be different, and the bullying they often suffered in consequence; the possession of strange mental powers appealed to him firstly as a way of modelling and melodramatizing that experience, and secondly as an ideative foundation-stone on which he could build compelling redemptive miracles. Campbell wanted the *psi*-stories which he published to aim towards the point at which such powers would beome the property of competent, right-thinking men who would apply them as a technical skill; Sturgeon, by contrast, aimed his at the spectacular salvation of the lonely, the crippled, and the deprived. Campbell wanted to plan the marriage of human society and superhumanity from consummation to completion; Sturgeon was primarily interested in the courtship to which consummation provided a climax and a terminus.

Psi-powers were not the only ideative framework which Sturgeon used in constructing parables of alienation and its transcendence. He wrote strange biological fantasies like "The Deadly Ratio" (1948; also known as "It Wasn't Syzygy"), "The Sex Opposite" (1952), and "The Golden Helix" (1954). He also used alien encounters in such stories as the supremely sentimental "Saucer of Loneliness" (1953) and the taboo-breaking "The World Well Lost" (1953). His first novel, *The Dreaming Jewels* (1950; also known as *The Synthetic Man*), is a mutagenic romance in which alien crystals act as an evolutionary catalyst, their imperfect creations providing the obsessive misanthrope Pierre Monêtre with a set of carnival freaks with which to make his living while searching for their secret. The central character of the story is a boy who runs away from home after being brutally punished by his adoptive father for what the memorably-deceptive first line of the story describes as "doing something disgusting." Suspense is maintained throughout by the paranoid implication that the boy remains under a terrible threat from the substitute father-figure Monêtre until he achieves a maturity far more dignified and far more powerful than his rival's. (Monêtre is, of course, translatable as "my being.")

The *psi*-story which remains Sturgeon's most celebrated work is his second novel, *More Than Human* (1953), elaborated by adding an introduction and a conclusion to the novella "Baby is Three" (1952). It tells the story of six individuals, each of whom is a social deviant or outcast and each of whom is possessed of a single supernatural talent. Ineffective in isolation, these talents can be integrated into a marvellously powerful whole when the individuals come together to form an unusual but nevertheless functional "family." The telepathic simpleton who provides the initial linkage is replaced by a delinquent boy who cannot comprehend his situation, but when a psychiatrist enables him to do so he quickly comes to see its true potential. The "gestalt" is sheltered in its early days by a "mother" whose well-meant attempts at the moral education of its members are handicapped by rigidity and intolerance; once the boy understands what is happening, he prevents further damage being inflicted in this way, but the reconsolidated group still has to discover a morality of its own before it can be accepted into a community of its own peers.

A similar but much less complex story of paranormal opportunities nearly thwarted by the moral straitjacket of an obsessive mother-substitute is "...And My Fear Is Great" (1953). Similar figures crop up elsewhere in Sturgeon's work of the period, but they are not as terrifying as the freakish and excruciatingly hypocritical father-figures who are their counterpart. The nastiest of these are "Mr Costello, Hero"

(1953) and Heri Gonza, in "The Comedian's Children" (1958), who infects children with a disfiguring disease so that he can pose as their guardian and protector. Almost all Sturgeon's figures of evil are human, the great majority assuming positions of pseudo-parental authority; his aliens are usually benign, like those which he added to "Hurricane Trio" (1955)—originally written as a mundane story when he was trying to break into higher paying markets—to play the part of a moral *deus ex machina*. Even those aliens which are not benign often end up doing more good than harm.

Alien catalysts which precipitate the redemptive development of human *psi*-powers are featured in two other long stories. "The (Widget), the (Wadget) and Boff" (1955) operates on a modest scale, involving the inhabitants of a boarding-house, and is somewhat reminiscent of Jerome K. Jerome's classic tale of angelic visitation, "The Passing of the Third Floor Back" (1907), which was the basis of a successful play and a film. *The Cosmic Rape* (1958; also extant in an abridged version, "To Marry Medusa")—a story on which Sturgeon apparently worked for several years after signing a contract in advance—is much more spectacular. It features an alien invader which jumps to the conclusion that the disassociation of human minds is a kind of facultative defense mechanism against the absorption of the species into a cosmos-spanning "hive-mind" which it has come to accomplish. When it sets about "re-assembling" the hive-mind which it assumes to be the natural state of affairs on Earth—bringing an assortment of frightened, suffering, incompetent individuals into a gestalt much larger than that featured in *More Than Human*—it creates an entity far more powerful than the one of which it is a part.

The difficulty which Sturgeon had in completing *The Cosmic Rape* quickly became more generally manifest. In an introduction to "And Now the News...." (1956) in *The Golden Helix* (1979), Sturgeon recalls that he had run completely out of ideas, and felt that he desperately needed some new ones in order to rescue his ailing finances; Robert A. Heinlein obligingly sent him a check to tide him over and no less than twenty-six story ideas (including, of course, the perversely memorable one on which that particular story turns). Despite the presence in his work of certain perennial themes, Sturgeon did not like to repeat himself. Unlike A. E. van Vogt, who had pioneered the kind of transcendental metamorphosis story which he brought to a much higher level of sophistication, Sturgeon could not be content to reshuffle old stories or recapitulate their imagery with slight variations. He always wanted to break new ground, artistically and ideatively—but his search for new ground to break became increasingly desperate.

Sturgeon's fourth novel, *Venus Plus X* (1960), is one of the few formal exercises in Utopian design produced within genre SF. The protagonist of the story is seemingly brought out of our own time to examine and pass judgment upon the society of Ledom, in which all physical and social differentiation between the sexes has been eradicated. The question at stake is, of course, the extent to which the difficulties and miseries of our own existence are generated by sexual politics, and it is outstanding among Sturgeon's work by virtue of the fact that it does not assume in advance that any disruption of present-day moral prejudices would be beneficial. Indeed, it is painfully even-handed, to the point where its very indecisiveness seems to constitute a profound disappointment.

By this time Sturgeon's work had become afflicted with a deep pessimism. All of the best stories he produced in his last few years of activity are heart-rending tragedies. Some of them are very fine, like the dying astronaut story "The Man Who Lost the Sea" (1959), but they represented a change of narrative direction whose effects were bound to be dispiriting. The novella "Need" (1960) is one of the best of his *psi*-stories, but it is also one of the most harrowing; here the possession of a superhuman sensitivity becomes an alienating force in its own right, and the self-knowledge which the protagonist gains by virtue of his association with the empath is coldly unflattering. In "Like Young" (1960), a vision of the evolutionary future suggests that it might—and perhaps ought—to belong to a species other than mankind. Most strikingly of all, in the brilliant short novel *Some of Your Blood* (1961), the hapless man alienated by his vampiric inclinations finds that his ingenious solution to his problem can provide only a temporary respite before attracting a more exaggerated opprobrium.

This phase of activity concluded, so far as science fiction was concerned, with the publication of an aborted novel, "When You Care, When You Love" (1962), which seemingly had not the impetus required to carry through to a planned conclusion asserting that love—aided and abetted by new technologies—might even contrive to conquer death in the interests of healing loneliness and frustration.

Sturgeon continued to publish short story collections during the sixties, including some previously-unpublished stories in *Starshine*, but such original material as he produced was mundane hackwork, including an Ellery Queen novel, *The Player on the Other Side* (1963), and a novelization of the Western movie, *The Rare Breed* (1966). (He had done such work before, but only as a sideline.) When he briefly returned to more significant literary labors in 1969-70, most of what he wrote was carefully marginal in its science fiction content, and most of it was aimed at the higher-paying markets he had failed to reach—in spite of his best efforts—in the fifties.

When the greater part of this new work was collected, along with the delusional fantasy "To Here and the Easel" (1954), in *Sturgeon Is Alive and Well* (1971), the author hopefully claimed in his introduction that this period of inactivity would prove—like the one of 1941-

46—to have been a period of gestation: "a silent working out of ideas, of conviction, of profound selection." It did not; instead, it decayed with remarkable rapidity into a deflated pessimism unillumined by the lyricism of the stories of a similar ilk he had published in 1959-60. Like the sickly fable "Brownshoes" (1969), the award-winning "Slow Sculpture" presumes that miraculous inventions which might alleviate many of the miseries of mankind are being suppressed by the vested interests of established industries and professions; the hope that the heroes of both stories might be redeemed by love is undoubtedly honest but dramatically enfeebled. "Occam's Scalpel" (1971), in which the inheritor of an industrial empire is equipped with an ecological conscience by trickery, is wryly conscious of its own sad absurdity.

One of the two long stories Sturgeon produced in this period, "Case and the Dreamer" (1972), is obviously another aborted novel patched up as a novella. The other, "If All Men Were Brothers, Would You Let One Marry Your Sister?" (1970) was written for Harlan Ellison's *Dangerous Visions*. Ellison was later to badger Sturgeon into producing another long story for his Shared World anthology, *Medea* (1985), "Why Dolphins Don't Bite." Both these stories are curious moral parables which suggest—with a wild optimism which is as unappealing as it is unconvincing—that Utopia might be just around the corner if only humans were capable of abandoning their ridiculous prejudice against (in the first instance) incest or (in the second) cannibalism. As a means of symbolizing the confining limitations of social mores and the dependence of progress on an open mind, this *modus operandi* compares very unfavorably with that employed in *More than Human* or *Venus Plus X*, and the extent to which Sturgeon had moved away from the Campbellian outlook which once ensnared him is evident in the insistence of the latter story that technology, however marvellous, can only ever be a consolation prize for human beings incapable of true community.

Towards the end of his life Sturgeon was endeavoring to lay out a comprehensive summary of his prospectus for moral reform in a long religious fantasy called *Godbody*, but the version of it which eventually saw publication in 1986—leading to a conclusion whose form is entirely appropriate but whose swiftness is absurdly premature—is but a tiny fraction of the projected whole.

Theodore Sturgeon was a writer of considerable eloquence whose best stories are intensely gripping; they force the reader to identify empathetically with characters who are as different from the stereotyped heroes of pulp fiction as one could imagine, and instill a fervent yearning for the salvation of those characters. The problem with any story which manifests this kind of artistry is that nothing short of a miracle will suffice as a satisfactory climax, and Sturgeon was too wise and too honest to forget or permanently set aside the knowledge that it is all too easy for a writer to provide such miracles. He always found it more comfortable writing fantasy than science fiction—and if rational plausibility is accepted as a criterion of qualification it must be admitted that almost all of his so-called science fiction is really lightly-jargonized fantasy—but he did have a well-developed science-fictional conscience, which made him ambitious to do more than compose consolatory fairy tales.

All writers have godlike power over their imaginary worlds, but those who specialize in fantastic fictions also have a ready-made apparatus which allows them to redeem any situation with a casual flourish. Sturgeon was always suspicious of the corrupting effects of this absolute power, as all those who seek to use it responsibly and constructively have to be; his conscience kept getting the better of him, insisting that it was unworthy of him simply to keep on producing reckless and essentially false eucatastrophes to answer the problems of his characters. That conscience was probably the real source of his "blocks," and however much his loyal readers might regret the effect those blocks had on his productivity, we ought at least to consider the possibility that had he been capable of doing things differently he would have been a poorer writer and a less admirable man.

X.

THE LOST PIONEER

THE SCIENCE FICTION OF STANLEY G. WEINBAUM

Stanley G. Weinbaum was perhaps the most remarkable of all the writers recruited by Hugo Gernsback to the fledgling pulp *genre* of science fiction. By the time he turned his attention to the SF pulps they had been in existence for eight years, but once his first story, "A Martian Odyssey," had appeared in the July 1934 issue of *Wonder Stories*, he threw himself into the wholesale production of similar materials. Seventeen months later he was dead, struck down by throat cancer at the age of thirty-three, but within that interval he made a deep impression. "A Martian Odyssey" was one of a handful of landmark stories whose publication brought about an instant change in attitude to one of the central motifs of the new genre, and the work Weinbaum left behind at his death offers abundant testimony to support the proposition that had he lived he would have become the leading writer in the field and a major force in its evolution.

Weinbaum was born in Louisville, Kentucky in 1902. He graduated from the University of Wisconsin in 1923 with a degree in chemical engineering, but his principal ambition was to be a writer. He wrote several novels in the twenties and early thirties but published only one, a serialized love story called *The Lady Dances* signed "Marge Stanley" (his wife's name was Margaret).

One of the early novels was a horror/SF hybrid originally titled *The Mad Brain*, which was eventually published from one of the specialist SF publishers in 1950 as *The Dark Other*. Weinbaum's first biographer, Sam Moskowitz, initially took the view that his only full-length SF novel, *The New Adam*, was also written before Weinbaum turned his attention to the pulps, but his subsequent researches led him to change his mind. In the Fall 1991 *Fantasy Commentator* Moskowitz suggests that a projected "superman story" which Weinbaum had discussed with Ralph Milne Farley in December 1934 must have been *The New Adam*. If so, Weinbaum's productivity during the last few months of his life must have been prodigious.

THE LOST PIONEER: STANLEY G. WEINBAUM

The Dark Other is a Jekyll-and-Hyde story whose hero has a sub-cerebral tumor which is actually a brain in miniature housing an independent personality. This premise could easily have been the basis of a melodrama that could have slotted into the pulp market with ease, but Weinbaum chose to develop it in the context of a love story. The story is presented as an account of a relationship which seemingly cannot succeed, through no fault of the parties involved. The father of the heroine, a scientist, ultimately finds an explanation of what is happening, but the *deus ex machina* which sets the situation to rights is rather unconvincing.

It is not clear why Weinbaum chose to develop such exotic material as a love story, although that was the kind of story he was trying consistently to write and sell. It seems unlikely that it was a commercial decision; even the most superficial examination of his meteoric career as a pulp SF writer cannot help but observe his constant preoccupation with hopeless sexual attraction. Although less evident in his short work, it comes out very clearly in his longer stories—especially those which, like "Dawn of Flame" and *The New Adam*, are markedly at odds with pulp formulas. In spite of the author's concerted attempts to pander to his market, it seems that the theme of doomed love kept asserting itself.

"A Martian Odyssey" is—on the surface, at least—a thoroughly masculine story. The birdlike alien Tweel is referred to throughout as "he," but in the light of recurrent themes in Weinbaum's other works it may be significant that the focal point of the story is the attempt made by the human protagonist to form a mutually beneficial alliance with "him," even though his thought-processes are so unhuman that the two can find few points of equivalence between their languages. The story was a revelation to the readers of SF—who were already forming a core community of obsessive fans, urged on by Gernsback's invention of the "Science Fiction League"—because it was the first story to formulate a picture of a whole and radically alien ecosystem. It insisted that life on another world need not mirror that of earth in any obvious respect, but that however different it might be, there might still be scope for intelligent beings to recognize one another and to form a tentative moral community, aiding one another against the merely animal and vegetable perils afflicting them.

This was a worldview radically different from—and much more congenial than—the convention which cast intelligent aliens as monstrous potential competitors in a universal struggle for existence, implicitly hostile to mankind. It is entirely probable that Weinbaum was not the only person spontaneously to discover this alternative perspective—Raymond Z. Gallun's "Old Faithful" (1934) appeared only five months later, and P. Schuyler Miller's "The Forgotten Man of Space" (1933) had anticipated it in one significant respect—but "A

Martian Odyssey" was such a vivid story that it made its point in a uniquely striking fashion. Its brisk and breezy style was far slicker than the clotted and heavily didactic manner which Gernsback and his successor as editor of *Amazing Stories*, T. O'Conor Sloane, had fostered hitherto. This new lightness of tone was to be swiftly and widely copied.

Weinbaum followed "A Martian Odyssey" with "The Circle of Zero," a tale of precognitive visions with rather pompous philosophical overtones. It was rejected (although it was eventually to be published posthumously in 1936), and Weinbaum quickly reverted to the formula that had already proved itself, producing "Valley of Dreams" (1934) and "Flight on Titan" (1935). His later work in the same vein includes "Parasite Planet" (1935), "The Lotus Eaters" (1935), "The Planet of Doubt" (1935), and "The Mad Moon" (1935). "The Valley of Dreams" was a sequel to "A Martian Odyssey," which likewise appeared in *Wonder Stories*, but the managing editor of that magazine, Charles Hornig, unaccountably rejected "Flight on Titan"; this and all the subsequent "Martian Odyssey" pastiches were sold to the much higher-paying *Astounding Stories*.

The best of these exuberant planetary romances are "Parasite Planet" and "The Lotus Eaters," two stories set on Venus—which is here assumed to keep the same face perpetually turned towards the sun, so that life flourishes only in the twilight zone. The second story features a memorable account of the fatalistic worldview of a highly-intelligent plant, whose destiny is to provided fodder for mindless predatory omnivores. These two stories and the inferior "Planet of Doubt" feature the same hero and heroine, whose ongoing romance never quite runs smoothly but is firmly cemented nevertheless.

Weinbaum embarked upon a new venture for *Wonder Stories*, producing a series of frothy comedies about ingeniously absurd inventions. The first of these was "Pygmalion's Spectacles" (1935), which was followed by a trilogy featuring the eccentric scientist Herman van Manderpootz: "The Worlds of If" (1935), "The Ideal" (1935), and "The Point of View" (1936). Although they are determinedly nonserious, there is nothing formularistic about their inventiveness. The first story features a kind of Virtual Reality, the second extrapolates the notion of an infinite continuum of alternative worlds, and the fourth suggests that the world might look very different from different subjective points of view; all these were early treatments of ideas which were to be greatly elaborated by later writers.

Weinbaum soon diverted his attention from this kind of calculatedly light-hearted work to a more ambitious project that was clearly much dearer to his heart: "Dawn of Flame," a long science-fictional love story set in a post-holocaust world. The world in question is ruled by the autocratic Joaquin Smith, and the story features an encounter between an unsuccessful rebel against Smith's empire and the autocrat's

sister, a *femme fatale* nicknamed the Black Flame. Apart from its setting the story has no fantastic content at all, save for the turning-point
of the plot, which ensures the impossibility of a romance between the
two protagonists.

"Dawn of Flame" was rejected because of the dearth of fantastic material and lack of action, so Weinbaum revised it thoroughly, expanding it to novel length as *The Black Flame* by adding various super-
scientific devices and a few battle scenes. It transpired, however, that
the pulps were not yet ready for a science fiction love story, however
elaborately decorated. It was not until Weinbaum's reputation had
brought him (posthumously) to legendary status that *The Black Flame*
was used to launch the first issue of *Startling Stories* in 1939; "Dawn of
Flame" quickly followed in its companion magazine, *Thrilling Wonder
Stories*.

Following the publication of "A Martian Odyssey" Weinbaum
had acquired a specialist agent, Julius Schwartz, and had made contact
with a group of local writers calling themselves the Milwaukee Fiction-
eers, whose leading light was the veteran Ralph Milne Farley, a prolific
author of Burroughsian planetary romances and a significant contributor
to the development of time travel as a theme in pulp science fiction.
Weinbaum and Farley collaborated on several stories for the pulps, two
of which were science fiction novelettes of no great distinction. Although Weinbaum was by far the better writer, he wrote the first drafts
which were then expanded by Farley—a method which suggests that the
older writer (perhaps with the best of intentions) was exploiting the
younger man's extraordinary verve. Both stories feature charismatic
anti-heroines, but that is virtually the only thing that marks them as
Weinbaum's work.

Either because he was so prolific or because he was frightened
of being typecast, Weinbaum thought it politic to disguise some of his
stories under a pseudonym; he wrote two as John Jessel. The first of
them was "The Adaptive Ultimate" (1935), the story of a girl suffering
from tuberculosis who is "cured" by a drug which enables her body to
adapt perfectly to any environment. She becomes a superhuman *femme
fatale*, and is perceived as a danger although she seems to be more
sinned against than sinning. She is treacherously destroyed by the man
she loves—who realizes too late the arrant cowardice of his fear that she
might have taken over the world. The story was later to be dramatized
for radio and TV; a movie version was released as *She-Devil*.

The ideas in the second John Jessel story, "Proteus Island,"
seem to have been derived from Nathaniel Hawthorne's "Rappaccini's
Daughter" and H. G. Wells's *The Island of Dr. Moreau*, but the more
interesting part of the hypothesis—the genetic engineering of an artifi-
cal ecosystem in which no two individuals belong to the same species—
is unfortunately subsumed by the less interesting sub-plot, which (un-

surprisingly) concerns a seemingly hopeless romance. The story failed to find a market until it was revealed to be Weinbaum's work, at which point it sold on the strength of his by-then-posthumous reputation and appeared under his own name in *Astounding* in 1936.

Weinbaum was already ill when he wrote "Proteus Island," but he assumed that his symptoms were complications following a routine tonsilectomy. He continued working at full stretch, producing yet another *femme fatale* story, *The Red Peri* (1935). This was a space opera featuring a glamorous female pirate which was intended to be the first of a series, but no others were ever written. He managed to produce only two more stories of his own—the last of his "Martian Odyssey" clones, "The Mad Moon," and a rather hackneyed space opera whose heroine is nicknamed the Golden Flame but does nothing to deserve the epithet, "Redemption Cairn" (1936)—but he never stopped work even when the true seriousness of his condition became clear. The last thing he completed was the first draft of a novella intended for revision by Farley which eventually appeared as "The Revolution of 1960" (1938), a curious tale in which a dictator's place is taken by his sister—who employs synthetic testosterone to sustain her masquerade—who then falls in love with the rebel destined to topple her regime; it may be regarded as yet another attempt to rework the basic materials of "Dawn of Flame."

A couple of minor stories produced before Weinbaum began to write for the pulps—one of them subsequently identified by Sam Moskowitz as a pastiche of a story by George Allan England—were rescued from among Weinbaum's papers. His sister Helen—who went on to produce about a dozen more stories for the minor SF pulps and *Weird Tales*, the later ones under her married name, Helen W. Kasson—completed one further novelette which appeared as a collaboration. All of these were, however, trivial works. It was the two stories of *The Black Flame* (which are combined into one in the book text of 1948) and *The New Adam* which belatedly revealed what Weinbaum might have done had he been able to evolve along with the rapidly-changing field.

The New Adam was published as a book in 1939, with a blurb insisting that it "far surpasses the best of science fiction." It was subsequently serialized in *Amazing Stories*—which had by then been acquired by the book's publishers, Ziff-Davis—although it was distinctly ill-fitted to the action-adventure policy which editor Ray Palmer had adopted. It is a thoughtful and painstaking account of the life of a superhuman: one of the first members of a new and mentally advanced species destined to replace *Homo sapiens* much as that species had replaced *Homo erectus* in the distant past. Weinbaum gives careful and intelligent consideration to the question of what the next step in human evolution might involve, and also to the problems which such an individual would necessarily face in growing up, effectively as a "feral child" in a society of his intellectual inferiors.

The New Adam was not the first novel to attempt something along these lines, and the evidence of the text suggests that Weinbaum had probably read John Beresford's tale of a doomed infant prodigy, The Hampdenshire Wonder (1911), as well as familiarizing himself— superficially, at least—with such relevant philosophical ideas as those of Friedrich Nietzsche and Henri Bergson. It is remotely possible that he was aware of the existence of a novel translated from the French of "Noëlle Roger" (Hélène Pittard) which bore the same title as his own, issued in the UK in 1926, but the Roger novel is an anxious melodrama in the same vein as John Russell Fearn's pulp extravaganza, The Intelligence Gigantic (1933; in book form 1943); Weinbaum's novel is much more similar to Olaf Stapledon's Odd John (1935), which similarly extrapolates the tale told in The Hampdenshire Wonder by having its central character survive into adulthood and encounter others of his emergent kind.

The first part of The New Adam describes Edmond Hall's youth and adolescence under the heading of "The Pursuit of Knowledge." A brief interlude explains his contemptuous rejection of the pursuit of political power and his commitment instead to "The Pursuit of Pleasure"—which is actually a eupsychian quest for personal fulfillment. This quest is, of course, doomed, not because of any innate deficiency in Edmond, but because the world cannot provide an apppropriate context. This part of the narrative is basically the tale of the protagonist's loving but ultimately unsatisfactory marriage: a union which cannot succeed despite the best will of both parties. Nor can this unstable atom of community be profitably traded for a relationship with the female of his own species he eventually encounters, although he does contrive to perpetuate their genetic heritage by impregnating her.

The New Adam is unusual in several ways. Its protagonist is treated with the utmost sympathy; unlike the Hampdenshire Wonder and Odd John, he is straightforwardly offered to the reader as a character with whom he (or she) might identify. Unlike almost all previous fictitious superhumans—and many that were to follow—Edmond Hall is not emotionless, although he does lack a sense of humor. Both these features anticipate the kind of superman who was to eventually become a science-fictional stereotype extensively featured in the pages of John W. Campbell, Jr.'s Astounding Science Fiction, although Edmond Hall's parapsychological powers are more muted than theirs and his ambitions more modest.

The two scientific romances which Weinbaum's novel most resembles—The Hampdenshire Wonder and Odd John—both include acidly bitter criticisms of contemporary society and the intellectual powers of contemporary man. The figure of the superman is invoked by Beresford and Stapledon in order to credit a special privilege to

131

those criticisms. *The New Adam*, on the other hand, is not so much a work of social criticism as an eccentric exercise in hypothetical existentialism. Like Nietzsche and his disciples, who were constantly on the lookout for the "overmen" among and within us, Weinbaum was employing the imaginary superman as a device in the search for better answers to the age-old question of how men should live. *The New Adam* is not an outstandingly well-written or well-thought-out account, but it was, in its day, a bold attempt to do something new.

One can only speculate as to what Weinbaum might have produced for John W. Campbell Jr.'s *Astounding Science Fiction* had he not been so unkindly struck down, but some indication is given in an autobiographical sketch reproduced in the omnibus collection of his shorter works, *A Martian Odyssey and Other Science Fiction Tales* (1974), edited by Sam Moskowitz. Here Weinbaum complains about the literary standard of pulp science fiction and the attitude of its writers and editors, but compensates with bold claims for the potential inherent in the genre:

> There's one general weakness and one universal fallacy in the material published today.... Most authors, even the best, seem imbued with the idea that science is a sort of savior, a guide, the ultimate hope of mankind. That's wrong; science is utterly impersonal and never points a way, nor is it interested in either the salvation or the destruction of the human race.... Science describes but does not interpret; it can predict the results of any given alternative actions, but cannot choose between them....
> Half our authors use the word "scientist" about as the ancient Egyptians used "priest"—a man of special and rather mystical knowledge that has set him apart from the rest of humanity....one visualizes either a noble, serious, erudite, high-principled superman or, depending upon the type of story, a crafty, ambitious, fiendish and probably insane super-villain. But never a real human being.
> As for the weakness.... It's merely that most of our writers fail to take advantage of science fiction's one grand opportunity—its critical possibilities.... It's the ideal medium to express an author's ideas because it can (but doesn't) criticize *everything*.... It can criticize social, moral, technical, political or intellectual conditions—or any others.... Science fiction can do what science cannot. It can criticize, because science fiction is not science.... [It can] quite

properly argue, reject, present a thesis, proselytize, criticize, or perform any other ethical functions.[1]

It is, of course, interesting to look at Weinbaum's own fiction in the light of these observations. Some of it he would doubtless have found wanting by virtue of its being slanted to the demands of the marketplace, but one can nevertheless see a continual insistence on the essential humanity of scientists and the essential impersonality of science, and an unfailing interest in certain kinds of ethical questions. These come more to the fore, of course, in *The New Adam*, but they are evident in the best of the magazine science fiction too.

The question of how men should live and what their best ambitions ought realistically and rewardingly to be may seem at first glance to be a more serious matter than the question of how men ought to approach alien beings and on what conditions they ought to attempt to form a moral commonwealth with them, or the question of how an extremely intelligent plant might regard the probability of its fate. It can, however, be very interesting—and perhaps potentially helpful—to reconstitute problems of how human beings ought to treat one another and how they ought to regard the fact of their own mortality as special cases of much more general questions about all manner of real and hypothetical beings. Beneath the delightfully entertaining surface of Weinbaum's planetary romances there are indeed serious issues worthy of the attention of intelligent people. Pulp science fiction improved by leaps and bounds as other writers carried forward his work.

It would be interesting to speculate further about the psychological basis of the near-obsession with difficult love affairs and *femmes fatales* which sits alongside the more rationally-ordered elements of Weinbaum's work, but there is too little information available to support any such speculation. Sam Moskowitz observes in his early biography of Weinbaum (reprinted in *A Martian Odyssey and Other Science Fiction Tales*) that he manifests a "powerful fixation on the concept of a superwoman who is tamed by love of a man," and wonders whether this is evidence of his "domination by a strong woman" or of "his subconscious wish to meet a woman who was his intellectual equal." Moskowitz—not a commentator renowned for his psychological insight—prefers the latter thesis, but is apparently unable to say anything about Weinbaum's relationships with his wife or his sister which might be relevant to this conjecture.

In an article published in the January 1938 issue of *Scientifiction: The British Fantasy Review* called "Science Fiction for Beginners"—of which the author claims, in *Astounding Days* (1989), to have no memory at all, although he re-endorses the sentiment expressed therein—Arthur C. Clarke recommended that anyone wishing to win converts to the cause of science fiction should start by providing would-be victims with the three best stories of Stanley G. Weinbaum: "A

Martian Odyssey," "Parasite Planet," and "The Lotus Eaters." This advice is now a long way out of date, but the logic of the argument remains solid. These three stories capture the very essence of the best pulp SF: they stare, in an innocently wide-eyed fashion, through the window of the imagination at worlds which are gorgeously and exotically populated, and which offer unprecedented opportunities for the exploration of all kinds of ideas.

Weinbaum wrote in a period when it was still acceptable to set stories on relatively hospitable worlds within our own solar system, and the disenchanting progress of astronomical science has converted his key works into an oddly nostalgic kind of fantasy; they have to be read nowadays as "period pieces." Even so, the reader who has the kind of imagination to which they were intended to appeal in 1935 is bound to have sufficient flexibility to experience them as they were intended to be experienced, savoring their glamor and their artistry. One has to make a mental effort to gain some sense of how spectacularly original they seemed at the time, but it is well worth making the attempt.

NOTES

CHAPTER FIVE

1"Revolution," in *Analog* (May 1960): 68.
2*Planetary Agent X*. New York: Ace Books, 1965, p. 83.
3*The Earth War*. London: Four Square Books, 1963, p. 130-131.
4*Ibid.*, p. 139-140.
5*Of Godlike Power*. New York: Belmont Books, 1966, p. 154.
6*Ibid.*
7*The Five-Way Secret Agent*. New York: Ace Books, 1975, p. 114.
8*Looking Backward from the Year 2000*. New York: Ace Books, 1973, p. 78.
9"The Throwaway Age," in *Worlds of Tomorrow* (Winter 1967): 158.

CHAPTER SIX

1*Poems in Prose*. Sauk City, WI: Arkham House, 1964, p. 38.
2*Planets and Dimensions*. Baltimore: Mirage Press, 1973, p. 14-15.
3*Ibid.*, p. 5.
4*Selected Poems*. Sauk City, WI: Arkham House, 1971, p. 103.
5*The Abominations of Yondo*. Sauk City, WI: Arkham House, 1960, p. 55.
6*Out of Space and Time*. Sauk City, WI: Arkham House, 1942, p. 299.
7*Lost Worlds*. Sauk City, WI: Arkham House, 1944, p. 63.
8*Ibid.*, p. 169.
9*Out of Space and Time*, p. 184.
10*The Abominations of Yondo*, p. 21.
11*Lost Worlds*, p. 213.
12*The Abominations of Yondo*, p. 42.
13*Lost Worlds*, p. 296.

CHAPTER EIGHT

1*Science Wonder Stories* (June 1929): 69.

Chapter Ten

1*A Martian Odyssey and Other Science Fiction Tales: The Collected Short Stories of Stanley G. Weinbaum.* Westport, CT: Hyperion Press, 1974, p. xxv-xxviii.

SELECTED BIBLIOGRAPHY

Brackett, Leigh. *The Best of Leigh Brackett*, edited by Edmond Hamilton. New York: Ballantine Books, 1977.
Dick, Philip K. *The Man in the High Castle*. New York: G. P. Putnam's Sons, 1962.
___. *A Scanner Darkly*. Garden City, NY: Doubleday & Co., 1977.
Hamilton, Edmond. *The Best of Edmond Hamilton*, edited by Leigh Brackett. New York, Ballantine Books, 1977.
Keller, David H. *Life Everlasting and Other Tales of Fantasy and Horror*. Newark, NJ: Avalon Co., 1947.
Malzberg, Barry N. *Beyond Apollo*. New York: Random House, 1972.
___. *The Day of the Burning*. New York: Ace Books, 1974.
___. *Final War and Other Fantasies*. New York: Ace Books, 1969.
___. *Galaxies*. New York: Pyramid Books, 1975.
___. *Screen*. New York: Olympia Press, 1968.
___. *Tactics of Conquest*. New York: Pyramid Books, 1974.
___. *Underlay*. New York: Avon, 1974.
Reynolds, Mack. *After Utopia*. New York: Ace Books, 1977.
___. *Blackman's Burden*. New York: Ace Books, 1972.
___. *The Earth War*. New York: Pyramid Books, 1963.
___. *The Five-Way Secret Agent*. New York: Ace Books, 1975.
___. *Looking Backward from the Year 2000*. New York: Ace Books, 1973.
___. *Mercenary from Tomorrow*. New York: Ace Books, 1968.
___. *Of Godlike Power*. New York: Belmont Books, 1966.
___. *Perchance to Dream*. New York: Ace Books, 1977.
___. *Planetary Agent X*. New York: Ace Books, 1965.
___. *Rolltown*. New York: Ace Books, 1976.
___. *Time Gladiator*. London: Four Square Books, 1966.
Silverberg, Robert. *The Book of Skulls*. New York: Charles Scribner's Sons, 1972.
___. *Downward to the Earth*. Garden City, NY: Doubleday & Co., 1970.
___. *Dying Inside*. New York: Charles Scribner's Sons, 1972.
___. *Hawksbill Station*. Garden City, NY: Doubleday & Co., 1968.
___. *The Man in the Maze*. New York: Avon, 1969.
___. *The Masks of Time*. New York: Ballantine Books, 1968.
___. *Master of Life and Death*. New York: Ace Books, 1957.
___. *Recalled to Life*. New York: Lancer Books, 1962.
___. *Son of Man*. New York: Ballantine Books, 1971.
___. *Thorns*. New York: Ballantine Books, 1967.
___. *A Time of Changes*. Garden City, NY: Nelson Doubleday, 1971.
___. *Tower of Glass*. New York: Charles Scribner's Sons, 1970.
___. *The World Inside*. Garden City, NY: Doubleday & Co., 1971.
Smith, Clark Ashton. *The Abominations of Yondo*. Sauk City, WI: Arkham House, 1960.

___. *Ebony and Crystal: Poems in Verse and Prose*. Auburn, CA: Auburn Journal, 1922.

___. *Lost Worlds*. Sauk City, WI: Arkham House, 1944.

___. *Out of Space and Time*. Sauk City, WI: Arkham House, 1942.

___. *Planets and Dimensions*. Baltimore: Mirage Press, 1973.

___. *Poems in Prose*. Sauk City, WI: Arkham House, 1964.

___. *Selected Poems*. Sauk City, WI: Arkham House, 1971.

Sturgeon, Theodore. *The Cosmic Rape*. New York: Dell, 1958.

___. *More Than Human*. New York: Farrar, Straus & Young, 1953.

___. *Venus Plus X*. New York: Pyramid Books, 1960.

Vonnegut, Kurt. *Breakfast of Champions*. New York: Delacorte Press, 1973.

___. *Cat's Cradle*. New York: Holt, Rinehart & Winston, 1963.

___. *God Bless You, Mr. Rosewater*. New York: Holt, Rinehart & Winston, 1965.

___. *Mother Night*. Greenwich, CT: Fawcett Gold Medal, 1962.

___. *Player Piano*. New York: Charles Scribner's Sons, 1952.

___. *The Sirens of Titan*. New York: Dell, 1959.

___. *Slaughterhouse-5; or, The Children's Crusade*. New York: Delacorte Press, 1969.

Weinbaum, Stanley G. *The Dark Other*. Los Angeles: Fantasy Publishing Co., 1950.

___. *A Martian Odyssey and Other Science Fiction Tales: The Collected Short Stories of Stanley G. Weinbaum*, edited by Sam Moskowitz. Westport, CT: Hyperion Press, 1974.

___. *The New Adam*. Chicago: Ziff-Davis, 1939.

INDEX

INDEX